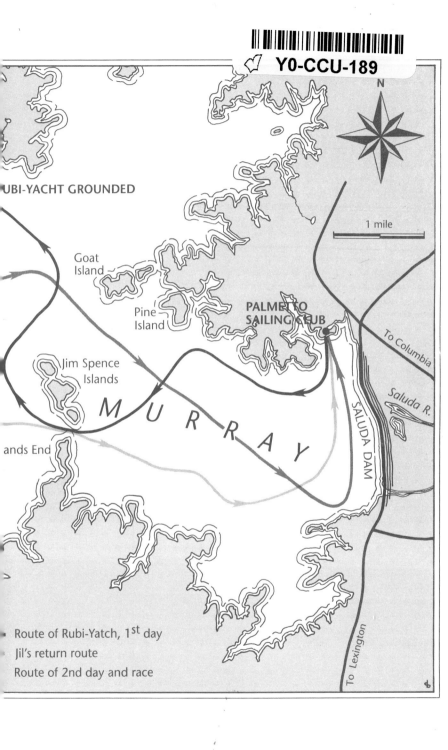

UBI-YACHT GROUNDED

Goat Island

Pine Island

PALMETTO SAILING CLUB

Jim Spence Islands

M U R R A Y

ands End

SALUDA DAM

Saluda R.

To Columbia

To Lexington

N

1 mile

Route of Rubi-Yatch, 1ˢᵗ day
Jil's return route
Route of 2nd day and race

CORBIN'S RUBI-YACHT

Benjamin Wirt Farley

Sandlapper Publishing, Inc.
Orangeburg, South Carolina

Design by Delmer L. Roberts

Library of Congress Cataloging-in-Publication Data
ISBN 0-87844-111-5

FIRST EDITION

for
FRANK and ANN

acknowledgments

The author expresses appreciation to the following publishers for permission to quote from their lists:

The lines from "An Irish Airman Foresees His Death" are reprinted with permission of Macmillan Publishing Company from *The Poems of W. B. Yeats: A New Edition*, edited by Richard J. Finneran. Copyright 1919 by Macmillan Publishing Company, renewed 1947 by Bertha Georgie Yeats. The lines from "The Circus Animals' Desertion" are reprinted with permission of Macmillan Publishing Company from *The Poems of W. B. Yeats; A New Edition*, edited by Richard J. Finneran. Copyright 1940 by Georgie Yeats, renewed 1968 by Bertha Georgie Yeats, Michael Butler Yeats, and Anne Yeats. The lines from the "Ballad of the Goodly Fere" are reprinted with permission of New Directions from Ezra Pound's *Personae*. Copyright 1926 by Ezra Pound.

The author also wishes to express his appreciation to the officials of the Norwegian Embassy, Washington, D.C. for permission to quote from the Norwegian national anthem, composed by Björnsterne Björnsson and rendered into English by G. M. Gathorne-Hardy.

preface

The idea for *Corbin's Rubi-Yacht* was born in an invitation to go sailing aboard the *Antara* on South Carolina's Lake Murray. Without that invitation and subsequent sails, the idea for the novel would never have taken form. I am deeply grateful to Frank Handal, of Sandlapper Publishing, Inc., for extending that invitation and for the many hours he set aside to help me understand the terms and maneuvers involved in sailing a sloop such as the *Rubi-Yacht*.

I am also grateful to others whose advice I sought and who volunteered to help me: Tom Waters, expert skipper and winner of numerous sailing awards throughout the Southeast; Lloyd Milligan and Christa Hunter, experienced sailors, whose reading of the first drafts helped me improve it immeasurably; Bright A. Lowry, III, professor of Chemistry and Astronomy, Erskine College; Judy Lowry (RN); George C. Wilson, former Air Force officer and Vietnam veteran; James Plaxco of Columbia; and Paul Agnew, attorney at law, Abbeville, South Carolina.

To Frank, his wife, Ann, and to each of the above, I will always be grateful.

chapter **one**

It felt good to be under sail again. Invigorating. Cathartic.

A strong steady wind blew across the lake and struck Corbin's sails near a close haul. It bore briskly out of the southeast and, as it rushed past his ears, created the sensation of sailing at a much faster speed than his *Rubi-Yacht* actually hauled.

Overhead the sky filled with large, drifting cumulus clouds. They lumbered along, crowding the sky with their billowing splendor, each uniformly gray on the bottom and flattened at the same atmospheric level.

Working to windward generated a profound satisfaction. The sail, at last, provided that sense of exhilaration that had eluded Corbin since tacking past the Spence Islands earlier that morning.

Corbin sat on the port bench, with his face and left shoulder braced to windward, working the tiller slowly and steadily and with a deftness that only time and experience could bestow.

Both jib and mainsail were set to starboard. Only occasionally did Corbin lean to his right and tighten or relax the pressure on the jib sheet. He could hear the gurgle of the eddies behind the transom, as the echo reverberated quietly up the drainline under the cockpit floor.

The sun had climbed to the height of its afternoon apogee and baked his face and neck with the full brunt of its August heat.

Corbin rose slowly out of the bench and, unfolding the tiller's extension arm, leaned forward toward the galley and peered inside the cabin. There, hanging on its hook near the boat's radio, dangled his cap. It was a skipper's cap, which he despised, but it was better than sunburn.

Corbin glanced about and, spotting the end of the starboard sheet on the seat to his right, tied it to the handle of the tiller's extension. He bent forward— rope in hand—and inched his way toward the galley, then reached inside for the cap. He returned to the stern and took his seat again by the tiller.

To the west, the lake shimmered in a molten glimmer, while windward and east, the water lapped in rolling crests of slate and blue and gray. Waves rose and fell in magical syncopation, one after the other, at rhythmic intervals. It was a good breeze.

The main halyard rattled against the mast and the

orange telltale ribbons danced perpendicular in the wind. Swell after swell of rolling water thumped against the bow and sloshed along the hull. The *Rubi-Yacht* heeled moderately and sighed to the tambourine sound of the wire halyard clacking against the mast.

> *A-roving, a-roving, a-roving's now my ruling;*
> *Alas, O love, my darling, a-roving must I go.*

Sometimes when he and Janet had sailed with her father, God Boy would contract a certain glint in his eye, cock his head just so, and begin to sing. That had especially been true that June when they sailed to Nova Scotia.

The sea between Prince Edward Island and the coast of Nova Scotia had rolled green in foam; white eddies churned amid the blue sea; waves slapped the *Nightstar's* hull and spilled across its decks. And wind, whipping across the whitecaps, had hissed the sea's cold spew against the sails.

Then, as the heaving and yawing of the boat had increased, it was as if something subliminal had burst to the surface in the big red-bearded man, and, assigning the wheel to Janet, he made his way forward, and, with the wind tearing at his hair, gripped the wet rail and sang for all the sea to hear, "Come away, hey! Blow the man down."

Or that time when the wind had suddenly shifted, rattling the halyards like tocsins, and the Captain had turned and, smiling at Corbin, begun to hum his favorite shanty of the sea.

Corbin held to the tiller and, lifting his face into the breeze, began to sing the words quietly to himself.

O there was a ship that sailed upon the Lowland Sea,
And the name of that ship was The Golden Vanity,
And we swore she'd not be taken by the Spanish enemy,
As we sailed in the Lowland, Lowland, low,
As we sailed in the Lowland Sea.
Then up stepped our cabin boy and boldly out spake he,
And he said to the Captain, "What will you give to me,
If I swim alongside of the Spanish enemy,
And sink her in the Lowland, Lowland, low,
And sink her in the Lowland Sea?"
And when the deed was done and back swam he,
We fetched him leeward from the reeling sea,
And rolled him in a canvas, for quite dead was he,
And we hove him in the Lowland, Lowland,

low,
And hove him in the Lowland Sea.

But the Captain had sung his favorite song only in the evenings. He would steal to the bow, alone, and, holding to the jib's stay, look northeast-to-east and sing an old Norwegian hymn. He swore it was the only Norwegian he knew, but he sang it with a noble lift in his voice and with a sadness—all at the same time. He would sing it in Norwegian, and then in English, and then in Norwegian again:

Norske mann i hus og hytte,
takk din store Gud!
Landet ville han beskytte,
skjönt det mörkt så ut.

Norsemen, whatsoe'er thy station,
Thank thy God, whose power
Willed and wrought the land's salvation
In her darkest hour.

You old Viking! Corbin thought. The man who had claimed his destiny. Now given unto the sea! And of your own doing, or "undoing," Corbin whispered to himself.

"Janet!" he sighed, as the reverie of her seafaring father faded, and the image of his wife took hold in his thoughts again.

"Corby, I think we should move," Janet said.

"Move? Whatever for?" he objected. "Surely you don't want to give all this up! Not after all you've put into every room, every floor, every wall? And what of the stairwell and the binnacle?"

"We can take the binnacle with us."

"Janet! Be reasonable! I like it here. Why throw all of this away?"

"Because I'm tired of it," she said. "I'm tired of living in the past. Tired of old Columbia. Tired of its old houses. Old streets. Old neighborhoods. Dying trees. I need a change of scenery. We need a *modern house.* Besides, everybody who's anybody is moving to Long Creek. And if we buy soon, we can still have our pick of lots."

"Darling! Since when have we ever cared about what 'anybody' else was doing or why?"

"I need a breath of fresh air," she replied. "That's all."

So they had put their house up for sale, bought a large lot in Long Creek, and begun building the "modern house" Janet insisted she needed.

It was of gray cedar, set deep in a woods of maples, red gums, dogwood, and pines. It came with a high cathedral window, skylights, solar panels on the southern roof, and a pagoda-esque hallway that connected the cathedral room to a den, kitchen, dining room, and bedrooms.

Janet filled each with modern furnishings: low sofas and settees, love seats, black lacquered buffets and coffee tables, and big gracious Oriental lamps, Persian carpets, and Japanese wall hangings. A huge gong decorated the wall above the fireplace, and peacock feathers poked colorfully from a brass urn. As for the binnacle, she set it in the middle of the cathedral room, under a Japanese lantern, suspended from the ceiling by a long black iron chain.

He should have realized her health was failing then, but he was too distracted. Too busy. With too many cases, even for a firm like his—staffed with five attorneys now.

It was early evening, near sunset. He and Janet were pulling weeds from around the pampas grass and its sawdust mulch, when he realized that the sun's soft June rays were not falling red or rose on Janet's face, as they were on the silky white panicles of the pampas grass, but, instead, were gray. He noticed, too, how pale and wan and old she looked. How frighteningly ill!

"Darling, are you well?" he had suddenly asked her.

"I don't know," she replied, turning and studying his worried face with those penetrative, exploring eyes of hers. "I just seem out of strength now, all the time, and out of appetite too. Would that God Boy were still alive and we could slip off on one of those long cruises aboard the old *Claire* again!" she smiled.

"You need to see your OB man."

"Don't worry about it," she replied. "I've already made an appointment with Jim for next month."

"Come here," he said, as he kissed her. "I don't want your eyes to lose that harbor glow. Ever," he said.

"One day they will," she replied.

"But I'll always see it. It will always be there for me."

"When I'm ninety, I'll remind you of that," she smiled, as she returned his kiss.

June lengthened into a hot July. Corbin had just returned from a law conference in Atlanta. He had come home late, to enter into the darkness of the hallway. The flame in the Japanese lantern glowed softly. Janet sat hunched on one of the sofas. She had been crying.

"I've had a series of tests, Corbin," she said, trying to dry her eyes. "Jim had to refer me to an internist. It's my pancreas. I have pancreatic cancer. Or something to that effect. Whatever it is, it isn't good."

"How do they know that?" he demanded, as if she couldn't possibly be telling him the truth.

"They just do," she said.

"Oh, God!" He moaned, as he bent down and pressed her into his arms and kissed her eyes and cheeks.

July melded into August, and August into fall, and fall into chilly winter.

Throughout that autumn Corbin had so hoped that Janet's condition would improve. That the tests were somehow wrong. That her cancer would go into remission. So too had Janet.

"Hey, I'm not a quitter!" she would remind him, her eyes filling with a soft smile. "Come on, now," she would reach up for him, hugging him about his neck.

"Indeed not!" he would reply, fondling her fingertips and kissing her lips.

But the sallow shadows in her face warned otherwise.

Then winter yielded into spring.

Sometimes when he would come home, he would find her bundled up in a warm blanket before the fireplace, even as late as April. Sometimes she would be reading poetry; at other times, fiction and philosophy. He tried to keep her supplied with whatever she wanted to read, however mundane, abstruse, or morose it appeared to him.

Once, when he came home, he found her reading Pound.

"Have you ever read Pound?" she asked. "He just cuts through it all with his haunting, restless images."

"In college," he said. "We had to read The Cantos."

"Listen to this," she said. "And tell me whose image comes to mind:

A master of men was the Goodly Fere,
A mate of the wind and sea."

"God Boy!" he replied.

"When I'm dead, Corby, I want you to inscribe those words on a stone and have it set next to mine, in memory of him. We should have done that long ago, at least have hallowed one spot where our memories could journey. Just for him."

Then came the afternoon he returned home to find Jil visiting his wife. His eyes searched Jil's as he took in the sparkle of her hair, the blush of her cheeks. He could hear the crinkle of her dress, feel the warmth of her presence, and smell the fragrance of her cologne. He sensed the power of life in her smile. That power and life that had so long been ebbing from Janet.

He walked Jil back to the door.

Janet had watched them from the sofa.

He had so much wanted to embrace Jil then.

So much wanted just to cry.

"I saw how you looked at her," Janet said. "She's very lovely, isn't she?"

He pressed Janet's hands to his lips and kissed

them.

She raised her frail arms about his neck and draped them around his shoulders. "You could at least wait till I die," she said. "But that's all right. God, how I love you! But I set you free. I set you free to do whatever your heart requires. To pursue whatever path you must."

"Janet! Please, don't talk like that!" he replied.

"Whatever my faults," she said, "I've always tried to be a realist, and I don't expect you to be alone for the rest of your life."

Finally, May came. Bright May. With its brown and gold day lilies and white magnolia blossoms, their aroma blowing in from the woods.

It was late dusk, and Janet lay in bed. The nurse from the hospice program had left only moments earlier.

"Corbin, will you bring me *The Rubáiyát*?" Her voice was low, dry, husky. "Please, read me the underlined passages." She held her hands up to him, as he sat on the edge of the bed and opened the red-covered volume. "It doesn't matter what order you read them in," she said. "Just read them slowly."

"I'll try to," he said, as he held the brass bookmark in one hand and with the other turned the pages to the poem's opening and began searching for the first underlined stanzas. These were the first to catch his eyes, which he read aloud:

> *The Moving Finger writes, and, having writ,*
> *Moves on; nor all your Piety nor Wit*
> *Shall lure it back to cancel half a Line,*
> *Nor all your Tears wash out a Word of it . . .*

> *One thing at least is certain—This Life flies;*
> *One thing is certain and the rest is Lies;*
> *The Flower that once has blown for ever dies.*

"Please, hold me tight," she whispered, interrupting him, as she lay her head on his shoulder. He turned and put his left arm around her waist and kissed her hair. "Please, read on."

> *"Ah, Love! could you and I with Fate*
> *conspire . . ."*

But Corbin could not read on. His heart was beating too wildly. Nor was there any need to keep reading. Her face had slumped against his chest, and her hands had gone limp on his arm.

He closed the book and laid her back gently on the pillow. She had slipped into a coma. He sat there and stared down at her wasted appearance. Then, still clutching the brass plate in his fist, he buried his face in her gown and wept. He lay there, clutching her gown and holding the tiny brass plate as he wept. "O Janet!" he cried. "Janet! Janet!"

Two days later, she died.

chapter **two**

Of all the boats Corbin Wright had sailed or owned, he prized the *Rubi-Yacht* the most.

Corbin had purchased the Helms-25 in 1978. It was a fast sloop for its class—a cabin sloop, able to sleep five—and measured twenty-four feet, ten inches, in length.

Constructed of fiberglass, the blue and white craft came equipped with a full complement of rigging, teakwood rails, and a sturdy, twenty-nine-foot, anodized mast, held taut by stainless-steel stays and shrouds that gleamed in the sun.

Its sails were made of lightweight Dacron, with a bold white *H* embossed on the mainsail, in a circle of blue.

In Corbin's view, the sails comprised the boat's most challenging feature, and learning how to trim them had taken him years and still required his best effort. When the ginny was flying smoothly, the slightest breeze would billow it full and draw the

Rubi-Yacht across the flattest stretches of water.

Corbin preferred, however, not to use the great Genoa sail, or ginny, as it was called. He favored instead a simple jib and mainsail and working to windward or sailing close-hauled. This he did, six to eight hours at a time, as weekends permitted, tacking slowly but steadily back and forth across Lake Murray. Especially was this true after Janet's death.

His sail had begun earlier that morning, as a fine mist had settled in the tall pines that protected the harbor of the Palmetto Sailing Club.

Corbin had parked his cream-toned Volvo in the gravel lot above the marina and had struggled out of the front seat. Having not slept well the night before, he nursed a persistent headache. He surveyed the sleepy marina below and the ghostly mist in the treetops.

"The mist should soon burn off," he told himself. "Or at least lift within the hour."

He cracked the window before locking the door, then proceeded to the car's trunk. He unlocked and raised it and began lifting out his gear.

A rustling in some nearby goldenrod startled Corbin. It was a towhee, scratching for grubs. Its dark brown feathers and black and white breast blended perfectly with the grass. Corbin smiled and continued unpacking the trunk.

He sat out a small navy-blue athletic bag, then a medium-sized Styrofoam ice chest, which contained sandwiches and beer. It was also stocked with potato salad, pickles, corn chips, and Cokes, as well as an ample supply of crushed ice. He set out a large, gallon-sized, plastic water container, then reached back into the trunk for his cap.

Janet had made the hat for him. The cap fit loosely, but comfortably, on his head. She had constructed it from remnants of a faded blue pillowslip, which she had hand-stitched to a frame of tan duck cloth. Corbin plopped it on his head and closed the trunk's lid.

He bent down and, grabbing the ice chest's handle with his left hand, managed somehow to clutch the gallon jug and athletic bag with his right. Then he carried the three items down to the harbor.

Corbin walked out slowly onto the dock, causing it to seesaw lazily under the cadence of his stride. As he bobbed along, he listened to a mourning dove's coo. He wondered why nature had endowed the bird with such a sad plaint. After pausing to listen to a second dove's mournful reply, he walked on.

He passed a dozen or so moored sloops, each riding quietly on its dock lines in the morning fog. Finally, he came to his own boat. He stopped to adjust his load, then straddled the boat's lifelines and stepped aboard the *Rubi-Yacht*. While its hull trembled in the water, he hopped down into the cockpit and rested his baggage on the port seat.

From somewhere out in the cove, an egret cried and took to wing. Corbin watched as the big bird extended its long white neck full length and raised its legs in carriage position. The egret flew gracefully and somberly into the mist.

As the boat rocked gently, Corbin leaned forward and placed his left hand on the cabin hatch to stay his balance. He unlocked and removed the hatch boards and stepped down into the galley.

The cabin was low, but deep, and was furnished with a dinette, sink, stove, and counter, and, beyond the main bulkhead, a V-bunk that could sleep two.

Corbin transferred his items into the galley. He set the ice chest near the sink, the water jug on the counter beside it, and placed the athletic bag on the galley table. He removed his hat and cocked it atop the ice chest.

The cabin's interior was somnolent, shadowy. Light barely penetrated it. Corbin sat down at the dinette, and, with his back to the aft-bulkhead, reached up and drew aside the seersucker curtains that Janet had strung over the portholes to his left. The blue curtains had faded an aqua-gray but still retained their fancy tucks. They represented the last touch Janet had added before her death.

Morning light seeped gently now into the cabin and illumined the picture on the opposite wall. If the table and bag had not been between himself and the wall, he could have reached across and touched the picture's surface with his fingers.

The picture was an enlarged, eight-by-ten color photograph of Janet and their son, Craig. It had been taken in the mid-seventies when Craig was still a child. Corbin had snapped the photograph aboard an earlier boat they had owned.

Craig held proudly to the boom; Janet had her arm around his waist. Craig was wearing a blue-and-white-striped T-shirt and faded orange swimming trunks. His blond hair hugged his wet head, and freckles crowned his fair cheeks. Janet was clad in a white blouse and white shorts. The sun had bleached her soft brown hair a strawy-white. Both their smiles radiated youth, happiness, adventure, love.

It was one of those rare photographs that somehow turn out right. It was the soul of the *Rubi-Yacht* now, and part of his own, too.

Viewing the picture suddenly, in the soft morning light, had caught Corbin off guard. He stared at the photograph for a long instant.

So much of life had slipped past. "Too much," he whispered to himself. "Far too much," he said aloud, as he pulled himself up and out of the dinette.

As he rose, he flipped on the boat's radio. It was attached just inside the cabin, near the sliding hatch. The radio was tuned to the weather channel, to which he listened with interest.

"Clear skies to variable cloudiness for the midlands. Possible thundershowers in the late afternoon. Current temperature eighty-two. Expected highs in the upper nineties. For the upstate and mountains, the lower nineties. Winds from the south and southeast, five to ten miles per hour.

"A tropical depression has formed off the south Atlantic coast. A storm watch is in effect for most of the coastal region between St. Augustine and Savannah, with winds gusting up to thirty knots. If conditions deteriorate, the depression will be upgraded to a storm. The Carolinas, however, are not expected to come under its influence before tomorrow, or early Sunday.

"Small craft are advised to keep posted for further bulletins."

Corbin flipped off the radio and stepped out into the cockpit.

It was time to cast off the *Rubi-Yacht*.

Each movement he was about to perform had its special meaning. Deep in his being he knew intuitively why that was so, or at least, suspected he knew. The ritual of casting off and sailing had become a solace, filling his hands with something to do and structuring his time with something to occupy his heart now that Janet was gone. "But who needs to know the whole of it?" he asked himself. That might cause him to stop sailing, which he certainly did not wish to do.

"I don't want this to happen," he whispered. "I don't want to lose this," he murmured, as he glanced about his own boat and out at the others, still shrouded in the soft white fog above the Back Cove.

Corbin turned to the mainsail and began to unsheathe its cover. His seasoned fingers moved nimbly along as he unsnapped the shiny blue conical tube that protected it. As the cover dropped off, he gathered it up and folded it smoothly to be stowed away.

He next turned astern to remove the smaller blue cover off the tiller. The tiller looked relatively new and still retained its hard coat of amber stain and glossy varnish.

Corbin stooped beside the sail locker and unfastened it. He raised the lid and reached inside, first, for the nylon jib bag, and second, to stow away the two covers.

He returned to the cabin with the pink jib bag

under his left arm, slid the fiberglass hatch to its aft position, and clambered on deck. Weaving his way past the shrouds, he crossed the foredeck and squatted beside the bow pulpit.

Corbin pulled the jib from its frayed bag, unfolded it carefully, and set both the luff snap shackles and head and tack grommets in place. He meticulously laid out the jib sheets, and secured them to the jib. He threaded the limp gray port sheet back cautiously along the deck, through the fairlead block, and looped it loosely about its winch. Returning to the bow, he repeated the identical procedure for the starboard sheet. Then he gathered up the triangular sail and tucked it against the pulpit. He retrieved the jib bag and returned to the locker.

After storing the bag alongside the two slipcovers, Corbin closed the lid, knelt with one knee on the hard surface of the sail locker, and, leaning far out over the transom, released the motor catch and lowered the outboard propeller into the water. He then reopened the sail locker lid and bent down to prime the motor. He squeezed the tank's black rubber priming ball several times to force fuel up and out and down into the plastic tube that led to the carburetor. Once more he closed the lid and, leaning out over the stern, started the motor. He listened for it to purr properly, as a thin iridescent bluish thread of gasoline and oil floated to the surface and churned in swirling eddies.

Corbin moved the throttle lever to idle and scrambled forward. He cast the dock lines off, hopped off the boat momentarily to guide it out toward the Back Cove channel, then reboarded, and settled down beside the tiller.

The *Rubi-Yacht* slipped quietly away from the dock. Corbin pulled the tiller tightly in toward his stomach and waited for the boat to clear its berth. He quickly reversed the tiller, revved the throttle up, and steered the boat forward.

He remembered his earlier headache, and realized that it was completely gone.

A lone rolling wake rippled outward from the bow and lapped against the hunkered sloops moored perpendicularly to their docks. Corbin watched the white boats' tall masts sway, and listened to the sloshing of the wave. He noted the many booms encased in either blue or green conical tubes, then increased the motor's speed and passed the lilting craft, one by one.

At last, he was under way.

chapter **three**

C orbin motored slowly out of the Back Cove and into a quiet bay. There he steered toward a tall white buoy that marked the entrance to the channel.

Floating beds of lily pads undulated in the water, as the boat slipped past them and skimmed across the bay's surface. More patches of lily pads crept out toward the channel and hugged the nearby shoreline to his left.

Streamers of dark green kudzu hung from the pines along the shore. A strong, fishy aroma permeated the air.

Corbin drew the tiller in and watched while the silent buoy glided portside past the boat. The fishy odor of the cove was particularly heavy, and he wondered why.

Must be the mist, he thought. The absence of a breeze.

He straightened the tiller out and guided the *Rubi-Yacht* toward the next channel marker.

As the vessel slapped quietly past the second buoy, Corbin noted that the mist had begun to lift. He held the tiller loosely and steered past still another buoy. He could feel the lake's tug behind the boat as the dark water purled gently against the rudder.

He longed for Janet and wished she were with him.

He longed for Jil and wished she was his. His mind began to wander, as memories of Jil's cologne invaded his loneliness.

"Corbin, the tiller's yours!" the commodore had announced. The commodore, Harmond Coker, was young and deeply tanned with glossy black hair. He was a dentist and had moved to the Columbia area from the Chesapeake. He had been the club's commodore for the past three years. "Ladies and gentlemen, Corbin Wright! Winner of this year's Helmsman Award!"

A smattering of applause and a series of hearty cheers hailed Corbin as he started forward to receive the prize.

"Hear! Hear!" called his friends.

"Well done!" congratulated an exhausted, but smiling, competitor.

"Thanks, Aiken," Corbin said as he drew near the big man.

He liked Aiken. Aiken Hunter was Corbin's broker

and confidant. Aiken was huge, but muscular, and with an appetite for life as great as his appetite for food. The broker had taken off his shirt, and the gray hair on his broad chest glistened with sweat.

Jil, Aiken's wife, was standing beside him and suddenly leaned out and hugged Corbin. She put her arm around his shoulder and touched her cheek to his. Her skin was soft and hot but, because of the heat under the pines and the sweat on his own face, it felt cool against his cheek. He could smell her perfume: a delicate fragrance, and could feel her hair against his.

"Someone needs to kiss the hero," she whispered. "At least for Janet's sake. Poor girl."

That had been the fall before her death, a full two years ago.

"Thank you," Corbin had mumbled, relishing the feel of her lips against his cheek, while repressing the guilt he felt at her touch. His hand brushed against her arm as she released his shoulder. He wanted to kiss her in return, but he respected Aiken too much to do it. He did not want Aiken to read something into his action which he himself could not truthfully explain.

" 'Kiss him'? Kick him is more like it!" exclaimed a jocular but tense voice.

Corbin recognized it as belonging to Oren

Medlow, a realtor, whom he had beaten in the race. Not that he disliked Oren. It was just that Medlow could make himself so obnoxious.

"It was the wind that saved you," Medlow averred.

Go to hell! Corbin wanted to say. But instead, he smiled as he stepped past.

Finally, Corbin reached the club's canopy, where Harmond Coker awaited him. The polished tiller leaned against an open folding chair. The lake's bluish-green water lapped along the shore behind the canopy. Corbin could hear its surf murmuring before receding into the lake. A stiff breeze slapped the canopy's weathered red flaps against its stainless-steel support poles. From somewhere out on the water, a gull cried.

"Thank you, Harmond," Corbin said, as he approached the young dentist and welcomed his smile.

"You earned it," the commodore replied. "Here!" he said, as he placed the tiller in Corbin's arms, hooking it over his left hand.

Corbin shifted to the starboard side of the cockpit and turned slightly to his right to stare back at the point and the sandy beach area of the sailing club. He pushed the tiller to starboard and watched as the *Rubi-Yacht* began to swing about and point toward the open lake.

The mist had completely dissipated and the air was still. Only one more channel marker remained to be passed. As the boat slipped by it, Corbin leaned over the transom and cut off the motor.

The boat glided slowly forward, slapping the water beneath its hull and drifting in the dead calm. Corbin aimed the boat into its own breeze—what little it had created—and studied the thin orange telltale ribbons for the slightest sign of wind. But there was none. The tiny ribbons simply hung limp.

Tough luck! he consoled himself, as he rose to his feet and steadied his hand against the boom.

Corbin made his way to the hatch, clutched the grabrail in his left hand, and pulled himself onto the cabin top. He slipped past the shrouds and began to hoist the jib. Feeding the pliable halyard quickly through his hands, he easily raised the triangular sail. Corbin lashed the jib halyard in place and set about to hoist the mainsail.

First he fastened the wire halyard to the sail, then pulled hard on the mainsail halyard. The boom creaked and began to rattle as the big sail unwound and inched its way upward along its slot on the mast.

Corbin watched it rise until the boom dropped, then he locked it in place, and tied the halyard to its cleat. He stepped down into the cockpit and unsnapped the boom's backstay shackle. The boom could now move freely about, controlled only by the mainsheet and traveler lines.

"Not bad!" he exclaimed to himself, as he reached up and caught the edge of the boom for support.

"Ah!" He had yet to haul in the fenders. He had completely forgotten them.

Returning to the deck, he pulled up the two port fenders, near the bow, and the two starboard fenders: one forward, the other aft. The soft vinyl tubular fenders flopped along the deck, until he wedged each against a stanchion. He was careful to keep them free of his jib sheets.

Now he was ready to sail. Except for one last preparation. His hat! And the centerboard.

Corbin stepped down into the galley, unhooked his hat from the ice chest, and laid it on his head. He turned about and reached back for the centerboard winch handle. It was fastened, just inside the galley's passageway, to the aft bulkhead, near the floor. He lowered the board twenty turns.

"That should be sufficient," he said.

Then he climbed back out to the cockpit, knelt beside the sail locker, and, leaning out over the transom, pulled the motor up out of the water. He held to it, until he heard it lock in place.

"There!"

At last Corbin settled back and rested his right hand on the tiller. He glanced up at the shrouds, but the orange ribbons still hung limp, only slightly quivering, and that due to the motion of his own maneuvering.

The sun was fiercely hot, and Corbin could already feel its heat through his knit shirt. He angled his face away from its glare and, hoping a breeze would soon blow in, listened to the hollow sound his boat made as it rocked in the water.

chapter **four**

The boat had drifted for what seemed like a long time. It sloshed to and fro only when a distant motor boat's wake would roll against the *Rubi-Yacht's* hull.

Corbin kept the bow pointed south. The cove lay immediately astern. If a breeze did not materialize soon, he would be forced to crank up the outboard and motor out into the lake in search of wind.

About a thousand yards off port stretched a causeway, over which Route 6 traveled. The highway ran north and south across the dam's earthen wall. Finally it slipped out of sight down another causeway.

Corbin could see the grey rocks along the dam's nearest embankment. Even from a thousand yards, the rocks appeared jagged and imposing. But more important, Corbin searched for signs of wind, any wind.

Beyond the causeway, he could see the tall, brick smokestacks of the dam's power plant. They rose high above the dam. Soft columns of black smoke stole slowly upward from the giant chimneys before leveling off in the atmosphere.

A faint breeze ruffled the jib but only caused it to luff impotently. The air was simply not astir.

No need to postpone the inevitable, Corbin thought.

He cocked his hat back to wipe aside a thin trickle of perspiration. Then he mashed the cap tight on his head and turned sternward.

Once more, Corbin leaned out over the transom, lowered the propeller and shank into the water, and started the motor. He hated to sail this way. But it was preferable to drifting back into the cove.

Corbin let the jib sheets dangle along the deck-tracks and made no effort to trim the sails. He listened to the halyards clack against the mast as he steered the boat away from the north shore. He kept the throttle lever on low, propelling the boat at less than one knot per hour.

"A breeze will blow up soon," he assured himself.

Just off a point to starboard, a number of fishing boats had begun to converge. Corbin counted six. One was a pontoon boat covered with an olive-green canopy. Its aluminum pontoons shimmered silver in the morning sunlight. The boat leaned heavily to one side, where all four of its stout occupants had assembled.

Less than thirty feet off its bow, a tri-hull motor-boat had anchored, and its three anglers were busily casting into the narrow space between the two boats. The largest man in the party, clad in blue jeans and a red and white baseball cap, suddenly yanked hard on his line. The rod bent in a tight arc, and the man's line began to rise slowly out of the water. A large black and white fish broke the surface and slapped the water with a sharp crack. The other anglers aimed their rods away from the action while the big man played with the fish.

Corbin glanced at the four occupants in the pontoon boat. Only one appeared to be fishing. She was a huge woman in red shorts and a pink T-shirt; she began hollering at the three men in the tri-hull. "Get your damn line out of here! We was here first! You blind, or somethin'?"

The angler closest to the man playing the fish laid his rod down and picked up a long-handled net. He telescoped it out and extended it toward the taut line. He slipped it gently into the water, where a sharp black fin protruded. "Hot dog!" the man in the baseball cap sang out, as the two pulled up simultaneously and swung a large bass aboard.

"Shhhh-t!" the fat woman swore, as she raised her left hand in disgust. "Some people just hog in ever'where!"

Corbin smiled and steered the *Rubi-Yacht* past the two vessels. An obese man standing beside the woman looked out toward Corbin and shrugged his shoulders sheepishly.

Corbin raised his left hand in a casual wave. Then Corbin buried his face against his shoulder and repressed a huge grin.

These people of the lake! he thought.

The fishing incident had caused his mind to wander once again, to memories of his son, Craig.

"Here, Daddy, you bait it!" Craig had pleaded, as he handed Corbin the hook.

"Well, let me see," Corbin replied. "A worm. I'll need a worm," he had glanced down at the child.

"Daddy, they're slimy!" A spasm of shivers seized the child as he handed Corbin the bait can.

"Oh, come on, now. It's not that bad. Watch! You take the worm like this," he said, picking it up between his thumb and forefinger. "You slip the hook right through this thick purplish belt. Slide it under his skin like this. Push the worm up on the shank a little. Then poke the barb out again." A thin red trickle of blood and a stream of digested mud squirted out of the worm. "There!"

Craig eyed his father with suspicion. "I see," he

said, with a squeamish smile, as Corbin returned the baited hook.

Corbin watched as his son swung the line out over the creek bank and let it drop in the stream.

"Try again, honey, to your left. In the pool there, where the water's a little deeper."

Craig reeled the line in and swung it out over the deeper pool. The worm, hook, lead weight, and bobber kerplunked in the water—all at the same time.

Oh, well! Corbin thought.

Little Craig's attention was totally absorbed by this feat, and his eyes stared after the tiny red and yellow bobber, until it floated upright in the ripples.

Corbin so hoped Craig would catch the trout. It was the same creek in which he had caught his own first trout.

Corbin could still hear his uncle walking through the tall grass and see him pushing the Queen Anne's Lace gently to one side, as he traversed the boggy meadow. He was turning and motioning for Corbin to steal forward. He handed him the pole. "Shhh, Corby! Not too near the edge! Swing it in gently. That's right. Shhh, not too close, or he'll feel your vibrations. Keep your eye on the line. Easy does it. There! Now. Pull! Good!"

"That a-boy, Craig. Keep your eye on the bobber."

"Daddy, it's going under."

The bobber quivered, jerked, then sank in a ring of ripples.

"Take it easy. He's just playing with it, honey. Now, pull! Set the hook. That a-boy! You've got him. Reel him in. Real gentle like. Up and out!" he laughed as he helped Craig flip the silvery trout onto the quavering sod beside the stream.

Corbin could still see the child's face, flushed with excitement. He had hugged his son and kissed his neck, while the child baited the next hook—worm, mud, grit, and all—without hesitation.

The motor droned quietly behind the stern as Corbin passed the last fishing boat.

He missed Craig. Craig was in Germany. Part of the NATO forces. Committed to defending the Western Alliance. Whatever was left of it.

How the mighty are always falling! Corbin thought. *Das dritte Reich!* Its ancient Prussian baronies still assigned to Poland and Russia!

Corbin happened to glance portside, toward the sun. The huge regal ball glowed hot and orange on the horizon. It had climbed just above the great smokestacks but to their south.

From somewhere deep within his subconsciousness, a verse of Yeats' "Irish Airman" slipped free and, whispering its way into his consciousness, murmured its lines upon his lips:

Those that I fight I do not hate,
Those that I guard I do not love.

Corbin blinked and turned his eyes away from the sun. He wished Craig were home.

Corbin began to search with earnestness for a breeze. He was tired of motoring along and yearned now for the lift of a wind, with its snap and flutter in the sails. He studied the treetops along the north shore for the slightest movement, the slighest indication, of a breeze. He passed a dock where a mid-sized red, white, and blue flag was draped at an angle from a pier. But the flag only drooped in the heat.

He glanced portside across the lake, but the water stretched bright and mirrorlike, glassy and smooth, as far as he could see, except for the rolling wakes caused by passing motorboats far out in the water.

A shore marker bobbed in the wake of the *Rubi-Yacht's* passing, and so as not to run aground, Corbin steered the boat away from the shoreline altogether. As the boat swung southward, Corbin settled back in the cockpit and listened to the gurgle of the water behind the transom, to the whining hum of the outboard, and pulled the cap down over his brow against the hot glare of the sun.

chapter **five**

Corbin had been sitting in something of a mesmerized lull, staring southward over the *Rubi-Yacht's* hatch, when the first faint ripples of water had inched past the cockpit. Corbin looked up and out across the lake.

A dark patch of ruffled water waffled to the southeast, creating thousands of tiny crinkled waves, wrinkling the surface of the lake's nickel-coated calm.

Corbin knelt hurriedly beside the transom, cut the motor off, and, straining hard, pulled the outboard out of the water and locked it in its catch.

He swung the tiller arm parallel to his body and set the bow at an angle to the ripples. He glanced up at the telltale ribbons and aimed the pulpit into the breeze.

The limp jib popped with the wind and filled without luffing. The breeze struck across the port bow and filled the mainsail with a clap.

Corbin tightened the starboard jib sheet about its winch and eased the mainsheet through the block, allowing the mainsail to catch the wind. The sails puffed and strained out in graceful arcs as the *Rubi-Yacht* heeled, ever so slightly, and lurched forward with a lilt.

"Ah, sweet wind, Aeneas knew you!" Corbin smiled. "And all Odysseus's seamen at their oars!"

He loved Homer and all the classics—after all, that had been his major in college. But he especially loved the *Odyssey,* and wondered if that's where his first call to the sea had been born.

"Ah, Janet!" he whispered, as he held to the tiller and began to tack southwest across the lake.

"Sometimes, when we're sailing," she had said, "it's as if time doesn't matter." She had been sitting starboard, opposite him, with her face to the wind, her soft brown hair whipping gently in the breeze, and the sun bright against her blouse. "Why is that?" she asked. "Why do you suppose that's so?"

"I don't know," he replied. "Maybe it's the sensation of moving, or motion itself that neutralizes time. That numbs it. Maybe that's what Einstein discovered, long before he ever formulated it into a theory. The neutralization of time. The numbing of it."

"And we experience it," she said, as she turned and studied him with her soft playful eyes—always challenging him, baiting him, as if she knew the answer but needed him to articulate it for her. "We actually experience it. In this tiny boat. Which I dearly love," she added. "Even if it doesn't have a shower."

"You and your shower!" he quipped.

"It would be nice," she emphasized. "And would make the nights a lot more comfortable come the mornings." She put her hands out toward his and, leaning forward, kissed him.

The numbing of time. The neutralizing of time. The haul of the wind on the jib and mainsail.

Corbin stared out across the lake, dazzling in the sun's glare, and held to the glossy tiller. He listened to the water gurgle against the hull and felt the lake's tug steady on the rudder.

He had met Janet at a party aboard her father's yacht on Lake Erie. He had gone north with a professor from Carolina, from the law school, to hear papers read at a colloquium in Cleveland. The yacht was large and had a pilothouse, or cockpit, all of its own. Janet was in the cockpit by herself, standing beside the brass and glass depth indicator near the compass. She was leaning against the wheel and staring at the distant harbor lights along the shore.

"They make an ugly town bright, don't they?" he said to her.

She turned. "Only at night," she smiled, the soft lights of the harbor reflecting in her eyes and off her moist lipstick. She was wearing teal-blue slacks and a silky white blouse, with matching blue loafers and silvery lipstick. Her eyes were filled with an inquisitive magic, and her soft brown hair caught the sparkle of the neon lights that blinked along the distant shoreline.

"You're with Professor Hollman, aren't you?"

"My accent?"

She smiled.

"I didn't think it was that noticeable."

"It's not," she said, measuring him with her eyes. "I rather like it."

"Thank you," he replied.

"The night is beautiful," he ventured, not wanting to leave her, or break off their conversation. "I've always loved the night and loved the stars," he said, as he glanced out toward the pastel lights of the closest bars along the harbor. The lights were soft and faint, pink and green.

"Don't tell that to Daddy," she smiled, "or he'll recruit you on the spot."

"He isn't hiring, is he?"

"No. Hardly. But he loves to sail and is always concocting some newer and bolder adventure. Do you sail?"

"No," he blushed, fearing he had lost her interest now for sure. "But I'd love to learn."

She looked in his eyes and grinned.

"I guess you've heard that before."

"Yep!" she blushed. "But I like hearing it from you. Come," she said. "I want you to meet my father." And with that, she took his hand in hers, while every molecule in his fingers pulsated with excitement, and she led him down the steps to meet "the Captain."

"Where did you say you went to school?" she asked.

"Duke, first. Now I'm at South Carolina, in Columbia. And you?"

"Ohio State," she smiled, squeezing his hand. "You'll like Daddy. Come on."

There were many boats now on the lake. Corbin counted at least three sailboats as large, if not larger, than his. There were also many speedboats and fishing craft working the water.

He glanced at his watch. It was close to ten.

Far off on the portside, a speedboat hovered on the horizon. It caught Corbin's attention because of its stark silhouette. It appeared at first as only a black dot suspended in a bright bubble of light. But as the craft drew closer, he could see its distinctive features, its bow up, and hull half out of the water, with a huge rooster tail of spray billowing out behind it.

He watched the boat speed closer and closer, arc slightly away from the *Rubi-Yacht,* and pass a good hundred yards to port. The breeze was steady now, and he could hear the water slapping rhythmically against the bow.

The speedboat droned out of sight, its rooster tail still scattering spray and dazzling in the sunlight. Corbin watched its long slate-black wake cut finlike through the water, ever steadily gaining on the *Rubi-Yacht,* until it lapped gently against her fiberglass hull and gurgled softly past the transom.

About sixty yards off starboard, a Helms sloop, similar to his own, crossed his bow. The skipper waved, while its two crew members sat on the windward rail. Corbin did not recognize any of the men or their sloop. But there were so many marinas and boat clubs on the lake, now, they could have been from any one of a dozen or more.

Corbin glanced at his compass. He was bearing roughly on a course of 220 degrees. The Jim Spence Islands lay to his right. They squatted low and green in the blue water, except for the reddish clay bands of beach that marked them off from the lake.

A lone yacht of mahogany decks and hull approached from the south. A party of three men appeared to be enjoying drinks in the cockpit. Suddenly, Corbin realized whose craft it was—Medlow's!

—and, tucking his head starboard away from the boat, he pretended not to see Medlow and his guests.

The big vessel motored past, crossing in front of the *Rubi-Yacht* less than four or five boat-lengths ahead. Its wake splashed heavily against Corbin's pulpit and sent spray hissing down the decks.

Medlow was probably ferrying prospective buyers from site to site. "And bragging about his investments in the condominiums across the lake," Corbin mumbled.

To Corbin's relief, Medlow's party ignored his sailboat. But, in Corbin's mind, Medlow was clearly wrong for passing too closely and for not veering off to the *Rubi-Yacht's* portside, which the big motorboat could have easily done. But that was Medlow. A philistine, through and through!

Corbin watched the big craft motor toward Pine Island and bear left. He hoped that he would not see them again. But a persistent doubt nagged otherwise.

Corbin glanced up at the ribbons and at the wind indicator at the top of the mast. The breeze had held steady the entire tack, blowing out of the southeast with Corbin sailing from close-hauled to a close reach, and he had had to make only minor adjustments, easing in the boom now and then and tightening the starboard jib sheet less than a tug. He was still bearing 200 to 220 degrees, south-by-southwest.

High above, narrow skiffs of cirrus clouds ribbed the morning sky, while, far off to the south, a band of cumulus puffs lumbered slowly along the horizon. Perhaps they were part of the tropical depression, but Corbin hoped not.

The condominiums were finally coming into clearer view. The sun shone brightly against them, and Corbin could see how the architect had designed their gray upper stories and overhanging roofs to resemble weathered cliffs, and their lower stories to favor palisades of rose-streaked limestone.

A broad marsh of brown rushes, cattails, and savannah clogged the shoreline between the condominiums and the lake, but an inlet had been dredged back through the marsh, making the lake accessible to its new "cliff-dwellers." A marina was visible deep in the inlet, where its boats' needle-thin masts blinked faintly in the sunlight.

A white shoal marker loomed off starboard. Corbin knew it warned boaters of the shallow passage coming up between the last Spence island and Murray's southern shore. Corbin watched the buoy bob in the bright water as he brought the *Rubi-Yacht* around. He could see the orange sediment on the shoal's bottom. Corbin's new bearing was due west, with a compass reading of 270 degrees.

The wind was now to Corbin's back, forcing him to bear away through the channel. But since the breeze blew from aft to bow and port to starboard, he had only to loosen the mainsheet slightly and ease the jib sheet one turn off its winch to take advantage of his new direction.

Corbin settled back, with his hand on the tiller, and guided his white craft between the two points of verdant green. "Once through the passage, I will then aim for Lunch Island," he whispered, as his mind filled again with thoughts of Janet and Jil.

chapter **six**

The *Rubi-Yacht* had scarcely made it through the channel when the wind died. The jib went limp and the mainsail sagged. Corbin tightened the mainsheet and listened as the bow slapped docilely at the lake's water, while the sloop coasted westward on its own momentum.

Corbin continued to man the tiller, keeping the boat on its westward bearing, as long as the nylon ribbons indicated the boat was moving. Finally, the telltale ribbons drooped windless themselves. There was nothing to do now but wait.

Far off the bow, to the west, lay Lunch Island. Its eastern face was treeless, but its gentle incline was mantled with a bright green sod. Toward the island's crown, a bluish-black treeline arched gracefully up, across, and back down into the water. A thin reddish-orange beach glistened in the sun.

Corbin had hoped to make it his destination by noon, but he abandoned any thought of that now. It was close to eleven o'clock, and he had acquired an incredible thirst, but he hated to pause for either drink or food just then.

Corbin stood in the cockpit and stretched his shoulders and arms. The tiller had an extension, which he folded out, and to which he now held. He liked to sit on the rail and hold to the tiller this way. It gave him a limited freedom to hike out on the windward side, although this was not needed just now.

The water lay very still and stretched off to the north and west in mirrorlike fashion. It actually appeared mercury in color, rather than blue, gray, or slate.

Corbin knelt on the sail locker and stared down into the water. He could see his reflection on its smooth surface and the blue and tan features of his hat. He could even see his eyes. And there was something more. It was in his eyes. And on his face. And under his cap.

He took off his cap and laid it on the bench and stared again at his reflection in the water. He had aged. Though he felt no different now from how he had always felt.

"Corbin, take a good look at yourself," he whispered. "You are growing old. And Janet is gone. And you can't ever have her back. Except in your memory.

Don't you see that? You can't ever have her again. And coming out here on these voyages can't bring her back. Except in your memory. Ever again!"

Corbin stared at his image for a long time, and then sat down.

That meeting in the pilothouse had been in the spring of 1961. Five weeks later he was back in Cleveland at her father's invitation, "to sail the Erie with me and Janet. Boy, I think she likes you!" the tall red-bearded former lawyer—now executive of his own import company—had scrawled. "We'll be loosing our docklines June second, so don't be delaying us none," he had added trenchantly. "Will look forward to seeing you, son," he finally closed, with a touch of affection.

And affectionate the old man had turned out to be!

He loved being addressed as "Captain," and amused himself the first two days of their "sail" by scowling sarcastically at Corbin's lack of experience and knowledge of the sea.

"Son, where were you born?" he growled. "In the mountains?"

"Yes," Corbin had replied. "Near Asheville."

"Well, I believe it!" he snorted.

Then he turned and suddenly barked, "God, boy! You're not baling hay. See here, it's done like this!"

Or "God, boy! Can't you do anything right? Watch! You crank the winch like this!" Or again, "God, boy! We're all going down to the sea! No, no! Like this!" But Corbin had always felt the old man's smile beneath his gruff imperatives and flaming smudge of a beard.

Soon Corbin came to think of the Captain as "God Boy," and would whisper that to himself whenever the old man wasn't about.

"Janet, I've got a new name for your father," he told her. "I hope you won't be offended—'God Boy'!" he said, afraid she might object.

" 'Offended'? I think it's marvelous!" she shrieked. "It fits him to a tee!"

And so God Boy it became, but only between the two of them, and ever as a name they cherished.

The boat itself was of Norwegian vintage—a schooner of Scandinavian birch and fir—admirably rigged and outfitted with ample sails and supple halyard. Broad of bow, the *Nightstar* had been built to muscle the massive, ice swells and swift currents of the North Sea.

"Had a cracked mast when I bought her," the Captain boasted. "And barnacles belted about her waist to the water line. She was a sad sight of a craft! But look at her now!"

It was dusk on the fifth night out that Corbin first

made love to Janet. He had not planned to. Till then, they had done little more than steal glances, touch fingertips, and kiss when her father was not looking. Then Corbin would kiss her goodnight, slip from the galley, and, squirm his way into the forecastle, where he undressed, showered, and crawled into his hammock in the darkness. There he would sway sleeplessly through the night.

Until the fifth night.

The lake had been rough all day, under a dark storm, and the *Nightstar* had been beseiged by the howling of wind and the spray of white caps. The two of them had hiked out since noon. They had tightened and loosened jib sheets and changed from main to storm sail so many times that they had lost count—and all the while both clad in sweltering yellow rubber rain gear. Toward the end of the day, as the storm subsided and the lake grew calm and the sun set mauve in a streak of smoky gray, Corbin glanced at Janet's hair, plastered to her face and head, and at her neck, wet with myriad beads of perspiration, and at her breasts, small and rounded beneath her white T-shirt. At that moment he fell in love with her. When her father finally went below to retire for the evening, Corbin kissed her neck and lips and breasts, and, rolling himself in her arms, which so eagerly received him, pressed his thighs and hands and stomach against hers, and made love to her on the deck of the rolling *Nightstar,* under the crimson canopy of heaven's dusk.

That fall he knew he could never live without her. And it was only his love for her and her steady stream of letters to him that bore him forward, impelling him to complete his degree and encouraging him to prepare for his bar exams.

"Daddy wants you to come sail again," she said, after he had called her following the exams. "It's off to Nova Scotia this time."

"Oh, no!" he sighed.

But he went.

And toward the end of the sail asked the Captain for her hand.

"God, boy! But you're young. The both of you are so young. And how are you going to afford her? What's your income, son? Do you even have a job? Good heavens, man! You have to think of things like that."

But God Boy consented in the end.

So Corbin married her that autumn in Cleveland. Aboard the yacht with the mahogany pilothouse. Beside the brass and glass depth indicator. In the cabin where he had first met her. And they looked out across the night at the magenta and green lights of the harbor. And she had held his hand.

Ah, God! It had been so perfect! So idyllic! If only it could have lasted longer!

chapter **seven**

That first year they had lived in a gray stucco house on Calhoun Street in an old part of Columbia. Built in the early 1920s, it stood two stories high, with third-floor dormer windows wedged between deep gables, and flaking eaves framed in white gingerbread molding. It came complete with squirrels in the attic. Towering magnolias shaded the home, and a row of willow oaks lined the sidewalk.

The oaks were old and were forever dropping rotten limbs. The trees' roots had buckled the sidewalk, and black dirt and leaf-litter had collected in the creases of the tilted slabs.

He and Janet had rented the top-floor apartment. It was furnished with pieces of what Corbin called "early black attic," furniture that lost its stain in muggy weather. Janet could roll the grit off the chair bottoms with the slightest rub of her hand.

"Oh, Corbin! Look at all this gunk!" she moaned one evening. "It's ruining every pair of slacks I have."

"I know. I'm doing my best," he said. "We're almost up to a thousand. Two more and we'll have the down payment. Then, it's skee-doo!"

"Well, the woodwork is solid," she rapped on the oak floor.

"And the rent affordable."

"Cheap, is more like it," she whispered, fondling his tie and pulling him down to her lips.

"Cheap? How cheap?" he smiled, slipping his arms about her waist.

"You should know," she kissed him.

"Supper at the newsstand? With chili and mustard?"

"How about lobster at the Palmetto Room?"

"With endive salad, shining in oil, and chilled Chablis?"

"Uh-huh!" she kissed him again, uncrinkling a crisp one-hundred-dollar bill before his eyes.

"God Boy?"

"Yep. It came in the morning's mail."

He was a junior associate then, with a large aggressive law firm. They represented half of Columbia's out-of-state auto insurance companies, two hospitals, a mill, a junior college, and a host of state agencies.

"Hey, there's enough business here for six firms," Corbin confided one evening to Slaygard, his colleague.

"Agreed!" his friend replied.

And so the two of them left to form their own partnership: Slaygard & Wright, and opened their new office in the old bank building overlooking the capitol.

"Darling, the firm's going to make it!" he announced. "Give me six months and I'll have you out of here and on York Drive!"

"Can you do it in two?" she smiled, as she wiped her hands on her apron.

"Two? Why two? I really need six."

"Because in six months, I may not be able to climb these stairs," she kissed him.

"Oh, no!" he half-blurted. "You're not?"

"Yep! I am!" she blushed, pleased with herself.

"Wait till your father hears this!" he hugged her.

"Well, at least maybe then he'll visit us," she sighed. "Especially, if it's a boy."

Which it was.

And he did.

When Craig was born.

"God, son! This is an attic! You can't live in an attic. Why, there's hardly room up here for the rats."

"Squirrels, Daddy. You're hearing squirrels," Janet corrected him.

"Well, squirrels or not, this is no place for either

of you, and especially not for *my* grandson."

"Look, Captain, we can handle it," Corbin assured him. "We just wanted to have the baby here."

"For sentimental reasons," Janet asserted.

" 'Sentimental reasons?' " the Captain blustered. "If that's what you wanted, I'd have shipped you the *Nightstar*. At least she carries more class than this! And her air, ten times purer than the must of this hole! Sentimental?" he scowled. Then with a hug, he embraced them both. "How I love you!" he kissed her. "How happy you make this old sailor feel!" Then he wrote out a check for three thousand dollars and flew back the next morning to Cleveland.

For the next two summers they visited him.

They spent the first yachting on the *Claire*—the craft with the brass and glass depth indicator—that had been named for Janet's mother, who had died at thirty, though Janet had never explained how.

"Of cancer?" he had finally dared to ask her.

"No. Of an overdose," she had replied, glancing silently into his eyes, then away.

The next summer they spent sailing on the *Nightstar*, with a visit to Canada, and passage through the locks of Niagara.

Other summers came and went. Janet grew tired of York Drive and longed to return to the older streets of Columbia, to its quiet dreamy streets, hazy with dust in the summer evenings, and heavy with fog on winter mornings. So they bought an old home on Wheat Street, in the twenty-two-hundred block, and began the renovation process.

It was a big two-story structure, with a French window in the attic, and a porch that wrapped around three sides of the rose-colored brick house. The front door was made of oak, with a large panel of beveled glass with intricate etchings on its pane.

"I love it!" Janet exclaimed. "I absolutely love it!"

"You'll have to," he said. "It will take months to restore it and a fortune to do it right."

"You'll be pleased," she assured him.

She had carpenters remodel the stairwell, turning the staircase into a banistered marvel of mahogany and brass, resembling the ascent to a captain's bridge. And along the wall up the staircase, she had enlarged photographs of the family hung: the Captain, Corbin, herself, and little Craig. They were set in porthole-shaped frames.

But she kept her *pièce de résistance* a secret, having it installed only on the eve of their anniversary.

"How do you like it?" she asked.

It was all he could do to keep back his tears. For she had had the carpenters install a binnacle. The handsome brass and glass post was set at the foot of the stairwell, with an elegant compass mounted under a glass dome, with both their initials enscribed on the compass card, along with the date of their marriage.

"It's extraordinary!" he kissed her, before he gave her his own gift: a pendant with a hand-painted likeness of the *Nightstar,* glazed on black onyx, with a diamond mounted on its sail.

Winters came and went. And Craig's little-boy years with them. And the Captain began to age.

The Saint Laurence Waterway had, for some time, opened the Great Lakes to increased shipping. Import and export enterprises appeared everywhere. The Captain's business fell off. He sold it, along with his yacht, and began whiling away his days aboard the *Nightstar.* Then one evening in late March, he slipped the old vessel out of harbor. "Am sailing her back to Norway," he wired from Halifax. "Will see you in June."

"Corby, he's crazy! Poor Daddy's crazy!" Janet sobbed, as she hugged Craig in her arms.

"I know," Corbin muttered. "Poor old God Boy!"

"What can we do?"

"I'll call the Coast Guard. Maybe they can help us somehow."

Then, three weeks later came the telegram. Dateline: Newfoundland.

WRECK WASHED ASHORE. STOP. RIGGING AND SAILS FOUND. STOP. BRASS PLATE, 'NIGHTSTAR,' AMIDST DECKING AND TANGLED HAMMOCK. STOP. NO BODIES RECOVERED. STOP. ALL SEARCH EFFORTS CANCELLED. STOP. WILL SEND BRASS PLATE C.O.D. STOP.

After that, Janet began reading. Always reading, and using the tiny brass plate as her marker. Sometimes he would return to find her reading poetry. Sometimes philosophy.

"That's bad for your mind," he warned her. "It will make you depressed. Moody. Come on, let's buy a boat! A sailboat. A boat we can handle together. And join a yacht club or something. We can afford it now. And we'll enjoy it."

"I love that idea," she said.

And so they bought their first boat—a fifteen-footer, with a twenty-foot mast, cockpit, and center board, but no motor, galley, or hatch.

They wrecked it the third time out. Corbin had named it *Claire*.

"I knew it was a bad idea," Janet said. "I knew it all along. We should never have picked that name in the first place."

Their second boat was a twenty-foot sloop, with a taller mast, and a hatch and galley. But the forecastle was small and next to useless, and the boom too close to their heads. Craig loved it and by age thirteen could sail it by himself.

They had given him the honor of naming it. *The Wright Boat,* he called it. He proudly painted the letters on it himself when he was twelve.

"Oh, that is tacky!" his mother objected. But actually she liked it. It was the sloop in the picture on the bulkhead wall, taken the week after Craig had named it.

Then came the Helms-25.

"Mom, it's your turn," Craig said. "Dad and I have had ours. But if you need any ideas, hey, I'm on!"

"Ha!" she laughed. But it took her weeks to come up with the name.

He had come home early one evening, earlier than usual. Craig had gone out with his friends to a high school game. Janet was in the study. She had flopped herself down on a big brown bean bag beside the base of a bookshelf, and had spread out several books in front of her. They were half-buried in the red shag carpet. She was hunched up over one of them, crying.

"I'm sorry," he apologized. "I didn't mean to interrupt."

"I'm glad you're here," she sniffled, blotting her eyes with a tissue. "I think I've finally discovered what I believe, really believe, and have for all these years."

He stood there silently. Not knowing what to ask or say.

"It's Khayyám's philosophy." She turned several pages in the book.

"I came like Water, and like Wind I go."

She quickly turned to several other pages:

"One thing at least is certain—

We are no other than a moving row
Of Magic Shadow-shapes that come and go
　　Round with the Sun-illumined Lantern held
In Midnight . . .

　　One Moment in Annihilation's Waste
One Moment, of the Well of Life to taste—"

She looked up at him with those penetrating eyes. "I love that," she said. "It strikes me as so honest. So simple. So true."

It was so nihilistic, he thought. But he loved her too much to quarrel over it. *"The Rubáiyát,"* he whispered.

"Yes. *The Rubáiyát,*" she said. Then she sat up, as a smile spread across her face. "That's it, Corbin! The *Rubi-Yacht!* The name for our boat. The *Rubi-Yacht!* It's perfect."

"Yes it is," he said, as he knelt down and kissed

her. Then he smiled and said:

"Ah, Love! could you and I with Fate conspire,
To grasp this sorry Scheme of Things entire
                              —and then
Remould it . . . to the Heart's Desire!"

"You, dog!" she said, as they both reached out for one another, and he, slipping his hand under her blouse, made love to her, there in the deep red carpet in the library, with the pages of *The Rubáiyát* open beside them.

chapter **eight**

A motorboat's low drone broke Corbin's reverie; he listened to its heavy hum until the drone faded and could be heard no more. A swell from the boat's wake rolled against the *Rubi-Yacht* and rocked it from port to starboard, before ebbing on.

Corbin felt very hot and dry—like one waking from a summer nap. He reached for his hat and pressed it down on his head.

The water blinded Corbin when he looked up and out across the lake. His sloop had completely swung about, now drifting from north to south. He was staring off to port, but in an eastward direction. Murray's southern shoreline loomed less then eighty yards off the bow.

Corbin glanced over at the compass; he was bearing on a course of about 190 degrees. He glanced up at the ribbons; the narrow orange bands were flitting silently from side to side. Just then, the jib flapped noisily and the boom creaked overhead.

Corbin checked the wind's direction and pulled the tiller in. The *Rubi-Yacht* responded instantly, the hull lifting against the lake's flat waves, as the bow swung gracefully and slowly starboard. The wind first struck the sails from abeam on the portside, causing the boat to point dead north, then the wind shifted, blowing in from across the transom.

Hearing the boom creak a second time, Corbin reached up and loosened the mainsheet traveler. He watched as the mainsail drifted right, then cleated the mainsheet. He leaned forward and, with his right hand, loosened the starboard jib sheet, then, with his left hand, tugged on the port sheet. Then he wound it carefully about its winch, until the jib sail fluttered portside and filled with wind. Finally, he swung the main to starboard and let out the mainsheet.

The wind came across the stern now. He could feel its breeze against his back. Manning the tiller deftly, he watched as both sails stretched full, and, settling back, he angled the tiller slightly to starboard and ran with the wind.

For thirty minutes he sailed on this tack, wing-on-wing, with his jib to port and mainsail to starboard. His bearing wavered roughly north-to-northwest, and only once or twice did he loosen or tighten either the mainsheet or the port jib sheet.

The Jim Spence Islands lay to starboard; they

formed a welcomed sylvan flank amid the lake's silvery glare. He could see the islands' green treetops stirring in the wind.

A young couple with a child had anchored their pontoon boat off the second of the islands. They were wading in the bright water along the island's yellowish-clay beach. They waved enthusiastically to Corbin, as if members of some lost expedition. He smiled to himself and returned their wave.

Once past the Spence Islands, Corbin turned his thoughts toward lunch: to sandwiches and beer. He was hot and thirsty and knew the temperature had easily climbed into the mid-to-upper nineties.

Beyond the last Spence Island a blue channel of water lay between the *Rubi-Yacht's* path and the northern shore of the lake. Corbin estimated the shore to lie about two hundred yards straight ahead.

The oncoming shoreline was part of Goat Island; to its right rose Pine—a wooded peninsula owned by the South Carolina Electric and Gas Company and which provided recreational facilities for the company's employees.

The westernmost tip of Goat Island tapered out into a point, beyond which lay the inlet to Ballentine Bay. Opposite the bay, a second point jutted out, where a barely visible reddish-orange shoal ran perpendicular to the shoreline. The shoal appeared to be a mile or more away, but Corbin singled it out as his new destination for anchorage and lunch.

With that thought in mind, he began the maneuver that would bring the boat about. He loosened the port sheet and watched as the jib sail fluttered across to starboard. The sail popped as it filled with the wind and rattled the halyards against the mast. Then Corbin tightened the starboard line and held the tiller fast.

His course now lay 270 degrees west, the wind abeam on the portside. The hot sun dazzled white against the big, bowed mainsail and reflected brightly off the hatch. Even the pulpit gleamed in the sunlight.

After completing the turn, Corbin happened to glance aft. There, knifing slowly through the channel, sailed a Helms-25, similar to his own. He could see its white *H* and distinct circle of blue.

Only one other couple had a boat so identical to his—Jil and Aiken Hunter. It had to be the *Columbia.* The sight of their boat filled him with elation. He watched as the *Columbia* heeled round the island.

"Jil, can that be you?" he whispered.

He watched the "ship" lean ever so comely to starboard and begin its jibe up the inlet.

"It's Jil, all right," he murmured to himself.

He could not be certain when he had "first noticed"

her with more than casual interest. He had always found Jil attractive, but never as "that other possibility" until sometime late into Janet's illness.

Of course he could be deceiving himself. Aren't all men supposed to be polygamous? "Women certainly like to think so," he mumbled to himself. "God knows I loved you, Janet, and you alone, right up to the end. Even with Jil in the room, you were still my first choice." But he did have to acknowledge that the thought of her had come to his mind in those closing days. "I swear, Janet, I meant nothing by it. Then, or now," he whispered aloud to himself.

But, in truth, he guessed he had "noticed" her from the first time they had met. Some twelve years earlier.

Aiken had invited Janet and him to sail with them aboard the *Columbia*. Until then, Corbin had never met Jil. During the sail they put into harbor at Ballentine and had lunched together at the little restaurant near the marina.

They were at table, having cold beer and club sandwiches.

Janet sat opposite Aiken, he Jil.

Jil had dropped her napkin, and he and she had bent down at the same moment to retrieve it. She was very tan and wore a low-cut red-and-white-striped tank shirt. Her reddish-blonde hair was cropped just about neck-length and swung straight and free about her neck and shoulders. Her blouse was very open when she leaned down and he could see the whites of her breasts where they curved in the cups of her brassiere. Their eyes met at about the same time and both of them blushed.

Thereafter he always found her interesting, though he tried not to think of her as anything more than that. Janet simply meant too much to him. Besides, that was during the days when they were renovating the old house and, following God Boy's death, learning how to sail.

Now he both wanted Jil and felt sorry for Jil because of what had happened to Aiken.

And though that had been over a year ago, it was still as fresh in his mind as if it had occurred only yesterday.

"Corbin, I'm facing a lawsuit. A big one, I'm afraid," his older companion had confided during a meeting in Corbin's office.

"I'm listening," Corbin said.

"It's over the market from last year. My client says I deliberately continued to invest in a sinking stock, lost him over a hundred thousand dollars, didn't catch it until it was too late, and am liable for it all.

"The truth of the matter is, I discouraged him from panicking; tried to buy the stock back at a lower rate;

only to have him insist that I sell it. And wham-o! He lost big! I mean big! And now he wants it back."

"We can handle that," Corbin said.

"Yeah, but all I have are the stock orders. No memoranda of conversation. No witnesses. No tape-recorded messages. No nothing. Just his insolence and anger."

"Who's his lawyer?"

"Some guy with Waither, Lockett, and West."

"I know them. We can work around it."

"I don't know. I don't feel good about it at all. I really feel sick. I've never been sued before. And Jil's as upset as I am. I, I," he stuttered. "I, uh!" he suddenly turned very pale and began to writhe at the mouth. "I," he gasped for breath, as his face twisted and grimaced violently.

"Don't move, Aiken!" Corbin said. "Just don't move. I'm calling an ambulance now."

But it was too late to prevent Aiken from sustaining a powerful, paralyzing stroke. Now he was in a nursing home, unable to speak, feed himself, or even control his bowels.

"O Corbin! What am I to do?" Jil had cried in his office, as recently as only a month ago. "Our investments are still sound, and Larry and the office staff are working with me, but poor Aiken. Every time I go see him he cries, and I cry with him. And then I come home and hate myself. And him!" she gritted her teeth, pressing her tears against her red-streaked face with a crumpled up tissue.

As Corbin sat there, listening to her, he realized how vulnerable she was. How unenviable and tragic her situation. And how beautiful, in spite all that, she truly was.

"What do I do, Corbin?"

"I don't know," he sighed. "But will you have dinner with me this evening?"

She looked up at him in silence. "Yes," she finally said, in a very low voice. Then she put her arms around his neck and cried some more.

He watched the *Columbia* sail silently up the cove. He had not seen Jil since that evening. Nor had he been to visit Aiken.

As the sails slipped out of sight, his heart dredged up the memory of that evening and clung to it with misery and longing. He had taken her to the Summit Club for dinner; they had had cocktails and had talked for a long while; then he had driven her home.

"Thank you, Corbin," she had kissed him on the cheek. "I needed that chance to feel human again." She put her hand up to his face, where she had kissed him. "You're a lovely person," she smiled.

He had placed his hand over hers and kissed her

nose, her lips, and then the palms of her hands.

"Corby," she whispered, "would you like to come in."

"Yes," he had replied, as he stepped in and she closed the door behind him, slowly and awkwardly.

Since that night, he had neither seen her nor called her.

"O Jil!" he groaned, as he scooted about in the bench and longed to hold her in his arms again.

Corbin stared off up the cove. "How I want you!" he said. "How truly I want you!" he whispered to himself.

chapter **nine**

O nce Corbin had tacked downwind across the cove, he collapsed the sails and anchored the *Rubi-Yacht* near the sandy bar he had seen earlier. He dropped anchor in about thirty feet of water—just far enough out in the inlet to allow himself drift space, but close enough to the shore to be out of the way of boats maneuvering in the cove.

He was famished and burning with thirst. He glanced at his watch; it was almost one.

Corbin looped the anchor rope securely about a cleat on the foredeck near the pulpit. Then he slipped his way aft, past the shroud lines, to the cockpit, and scrambled down into the galley.

He had not felt so hungry in years.

Corbin took his hat off and laid it on the counter, then removed the lid from the ice chest. The ice had only partially melted since morning, and its bluish-clear crystals and crushed hunks looked delicious as they were. He scooped up some to quench his thirst.

Slipping his hand beneath the iridescent ice, he groped for a beer, plucked one from its plastic holder, then pulled the can up through the hole in the ice which he had made with his hand. He was careful not to spill any of the crystals, as he wanted the ice to last all day. "Ahhh!" he sighed, as he held the cold can up to his face. He snapped the ring up and popped off the key. He listened as the pressure escaped from the can and smelled the aroma of the beer.

Janet had always hated it when he drank directly from a can. "Please, use a cup!" she would say. But he took a big gulp from it now. Then he opened the cabinet door beneath the counter and slipped out a paper plate, waxed cup, and a small box of plastic utensils. He placed them on the table, then poured about half of the remaining beer into the cup. He watched the golden liquid purl into the cup as its foam rose; then, bending down, he buried his mouth in the froth. The beer both stung and soothed his parched lips. Then, licking off the foam, he took another gulp.

Corbin set his athletic bag in the seat beneath the picture and turned back to the ice chest. Everything in it he had bought that morning at a convenience store in Irmo, just prior to driving down to the marina. He had placed one six-pack of beer and another of Cokes in the chest before pouring the ice over them. In the right-hand corner he had lined up a stack of ham and cheese sandwiches and a package of beef sticks, and around these he had wedged a carton of potato salad and a small jar of sliced dill pickles. Then, thrown in at the last moment, he had added a bag of corn chips. Now he was ready to eat it all!

He sat the potato salad, pickles, and chips on the table and laid a sandwich in his plate. He replaced the Styrofoam lid on the ice chest. Finally he scooted into the booth.

Bright shafts of sunshine streamed into the galley, past the curtains Janet had made. An unexpected quietness seemed to come over him and a sadness in it. From their sanctuary on the wall, Janet and Craig looked out across the table at him.

"Darling, let me take one of you," Janet had said. But he had waved it off. How he wished just then that he might put his arm around that husky child and touch his lips against the mouth of that woman he had so dearly loved!

Corbin began unwrapping his sandwich. Plucking a fork out of the small box of utensils, he helped himself to some potato salad and a pickle. He opened the chip bag and sifted a half-dozen or more corn chips into his plate. He took a long sip of beer and began eating his lunch.

About midway through his sandwich, Corbin leaned over and switched on the weather channel.

"Current temperature ninety-five in the midlands; highs today expected to reach ninety-nine; ninety-six in the mountains. Most of the state is still under partly cloudy skies. Thundershowers likely in the late afternoon and early evening.

"A tropical depression has stalled off the southeast Atlantic coast. Winds gusting up to sixty knots. A small-craft advisory is now in effect from Daytona to Jacksonville, Florida. A high still dominates northern Virginia. Until it passes, the depression is not expected to influence the Carolina coastal area.

"Small craft are advised to keep posted for further bulletins."

Corbin flipped off the switch and glanced past the hatch toward the stern. It was very calm where he had anchored. The wind had dropped, and only slight breezes rippled the water across the cove.

A lone cloud floated above the upper end of the cove, and when he turned to look out the galley toward the south, only a few cumulus puffs were visible at all. But far in the distance to the south, rose a faint, dark line of thunderheads, barely visible through the haze. The sun itself glared down mercilessly overhead, and the lake, all across the southeastern and southern horizon, glimmered in a bright, molten, metallic glow.

"It will rain all right," he thought. It was simply too hot not to. But he doubted that it would rain before six or seven.

Corbin finished eating his sandwich and poured the last stream of beer into his cup. The potato salad was too highly seasoned with mustard and vinegar. It glistened with food coloring, and the potatoes had turned a dark, yellowish green. Nonetheless, he ate what he had spooned out. He enjoyed the pickle slice the most, savoring its crisp crunchy texture and dill flavoring down to the last bite.

In between his last sips of beer, Corbin munched on the few corn chips he had placed on his plate. They were salty and left a light residue of grease on his palate and lips.

He considered drinking a second beer, but instead scooted over toward the ice chest, dipped his cup into the ice, and, after unscrewing the water jug's cap, filled his cup with water. He drank it slowly, finding it almost as satisfying as the beer.

Corbin gathered up his soiled plate and spoon, deposited them in a small plastic bag under the sink, and drank the remaining ice out of his cup.

He debated the merits of crawling into the forecastle to take a nap on its musty V-bunk. He was afraid he might fall asleep and not wake up for several hours.

Still, until a breeze returned, it was too hot to sit out in the cockpit or on the hatch.

There were books, however, to be read. Janet had squirreled them away before her illness. The prospect of the nap seemed the more inviting of the two choices, but lest he doze off, he began rummaging through the *Rubi-Yacht* for whatever might turn up. After several minutes of exploring the forecastle, he came out with a book of Frost's poems, a collection of American verse containing Longfellow, Whitman, Eliot, and Pound, and the second volume of a two-volume anthology of British literature. He also discovered a novel by Updike, a copy of Emily Brontë's *Wuthering Heights,* and two Harlequin romances.

"Oh, well!" he smiled to himself.

He blew the lint off the collection of American verse and wiped a line of smudge from the British volume. He stacked them on the table, sat down in the booth, and began to leaf through the anthology of British verse.

For a long while he reread his old favorites. Then while flipping hurriedly through the Tennyson section, he happened to skim "Ulysses." To his surprise, its lines spoke powerfully to him and rekindled memories of God Boy; he reread the poem a second and third time, though only its images caught his eyes:

Through scudding drifts. . .

> *. . . I am become a name;*
> *always running with a hungry heart*
> *the dim sea . . .*
>
> *. . . like a sinking star*
> *Beyond the utmost bound . . .*
>
> *. . . for my purpose holds*
> *To sail beyond the sunset, and the baths*
> *Of all the western stars.*

"Pop," he had addressed the Captain, "Why did you abandon the legal profession? What wasn't satisfying about it? The hours?"

"Hardly that," the big red-bearded man had growled.

They were aboard the *Nightstar;* Janet and Craig had gone below. Janet was trying to feed Craig his oatmeal papulum. God Boy was manning the wheel. It was late morning. The wind was steady, and the Erie twinkled in the sunlight of a million reflectors in a bobbing cobalt sea.

The Captain turned toward Corbin and smiled in his gruff but accepting way. "I suppose it was my destiny. Mine to claim," he said.

"My father was of Norwegian descent; my mother Dutch. They were Vandermeers. 'Wanderers of the sea,' my mother used to say. But my father had had a child by some Norwegian peasant woman on one of his return voyages home. We knew nothing about it until his death.

"Several months after the will was read, an official from the Norwegian consulate in New York showed up at my office in Cleveland; he carried a frayed black leather briefcase with him, stuffed with official-looking papers. He also carried a suit, filed in the district court, against my father.

"I knew it couldn't stand up in our courts, but I knew how much embarrassment it would cause for my mother and possibly my practice. So I hired a lawyer friend to represent the family in an out-of-court settlement. He botched the damn thing. We were charged with bribery and perjury before it was over. News was leaked to the press. My mother went into a depression and later had to be committed to an asylum. She died there six months later.

"After that I grew restless. Resentful, is more like it," he scowled. "God, but I grew bitter! I wanted nothing more to do with the law or with its courts. I wanted to get away. Escape!

"Vandermeer! I would become a 'wanderer of the seas!' I vowed. I took what assets remained of my father's business—he was an accountant for several shipping firms—and invested them in an old ware-house at the harbor. That launched my new career.

"I damn near starved the first four years. But then

I met Claire. Her family had money. And soon enough I was on the road to becoming an entrepreneur.

"Then I started buying boats." He smiled and pulled on his beard. "The first launch I ever owned was a tugboat. An old rotting buckling green tub. But one hell of a good ship!" he grinned. "Then I bought the *Claire* and eventually this honey of a vessel!" he slapped the wheel of the *Nightstar.*

"God, boy! I didn't mean to tell you that much. You are one, persistent, hell of a son-in-law!" he clapped Corbin on the shoulder. "And, though I've become sour on the law, the world does need a few of your ilk!"

Corbin glanced again at Tennyson's words:
To sail beyond the sunset . . .
Of all the western stars.
The Captain had not quite done that, but he was alive in this passage, and Corbin could feel his presence, if only as a distinct blur and remembered voice.

As he reflected on the Captain and the poem, he realized that there was only one modern voice that truly sounded his own soul:
Now that my ladder's gone
I must lie down where all the ladders start
In the foul rag and bone shop of the heart.

If he had a credo, those three lines of Yeats alone declared it. No Vandermeer was he. But there was a restlessness within. And those words of Yeats were like a manifesto; they constituted his understanding of humanitas.

He closed the book and looked up silently at Janet and Craig's picture.

"Forgive me, my love," he whispered. For now he so hoped that he would run into Jil again! "Ah, damn!"

Then he returned the books to the forecastle and made his way back out to the cockpit.

chapter **ten**

Corbin knelt on the deck of the *Rubi-Yacht* and untied the rope about the pulpit. He bent over the rail and briskly began drawing up the wet cord. Droplets of water sparkled off his hands as his fingers moved quickly along. The anchor broke the surface of the water, clouding it with a tinge of sienna sediment dredged up from the bottom. Corbin leaned way out over the pulpit and retrieved the metal weight. After securing the anchor in place, he scooted its rope and chain under the pulpit.

Corbin stepped back and cautiously straddled the collapsed jib. He stooped beside the mast, unfastened the jib's halyard, and hoisted the triangular sail up the tall aluminum pole. He lashed the rope about its hook and turned to haul up the main cloth.

Just then the sun glinted off the windshield of a large yacht, motoring heavily out in the inlet. It was moving slowly and heading in his direction. Corbin removed his hat and waved to it in a friendly manner.

As he did, the mahogany decks and chrome trim of Oren Medlow's boat shimmered into view. The boat veered slightly to Corbin's right, but continued its head-on course. Corbin could hear Medlow throttling up its motor.

What the hell's he up to? Corbin wondered.

Suddenly, the big boat's bow nosed up as its stern settled low in the water. The muffled roar of its engine grew louder. The yacht's speed increased and a deep trench of water formed ominously behind it. Water hurtled off its bow. Corbin could hear the thomp, thomp, thomp, of the hull as the boat raced closer and closer.

Corbin began to wave his hat frantically. "Damn! He's going to swamp me!"

In a flash of sunlight, Medlow's boat roared past Corbin's stern. Corbin could see all three of its occupants. Medlow was standing behind the wheel, grinning. His two guests seemed surprisingly unperturbed. They were too drunk to sense the danger. Spray from the big yacht hissed across the *Rubi-Yacht's* entire stern, cockpit, boom, and galley.

Corbin grasped the mast as Medlow careened his craft sharply to the right, to make a second pass, portside. Corbin braced himself for what would follow.

The first wall of water tilted the *Rubi-Yacht* violently, then smashed against the starboard side. A tremor seized the mast, causing the jib halyard to come unwound. At that, the headsail sagged and collapsed in a tangle of Dacron about the deck.

Just then the second wake hit; it slapped the boat in the opposite direction, sending a spew of spray high into the air. The whiplash slammed Corbin against the shroud lines and sent him—hat and all—cartwheeling backwards through the standing rigging and into the lake.

Corbin came up quickly, but his hat was gone. He could see it sinking in the murky depths. A wave, rolling back off the *Rubi-Yacht*, washed over his head and burned his nostrils. He opened his eyes under water, just as his hat caught the last pale rays of the sun's filtered light, then sank into the deep.

As he lifted his face out of the water he could hear the low murmuring of the big boat's exhaust sputtering softly behind him. Medlow had all but cut its engine. Corbin could feel the big yacht drifting up behind him. Corbin treaded the choppy water as the boat approached.

"Hey, mate!" called Medlow. His voice was worried, shaky. "No hard feelings, pal. Didn't mean to get so close. Here, let me help you," he offered.

But Corbin refused to turn his face or look up. He would not dignify his offer. If you were only alone, thought Corbin, I would drag you out of that boat.!

"Hell, I'm trying to help you," Medlow said.

Corbin continued to tread the water and move away from Medlow's craft.

"Hey! I said I was sorry!" called the swarthy realtor. "What the hell!"

Corbin slipped silently under water and began swimming toward the *Rubi-Yacht*. He could hear the big boat throttle up and drone away.

Corbin swam to the stern of his vessel and rested momentarily by the transom. He held to the ladder's rails until he had regained his breath. Then he pulled himself up—rung-by-rung—until he could swing his body over into the cockpit.

After another pause for breath, Corbin sat up and glanced into the galley. Everything there was topsy-turvy. He was just about to stand when the boat began to tremble. Suddenly, it hurled him forward, head-long toward the galley. Corbin struck the aft-bulkhead with his right shoulder. He tried to rise but a roaring, sundering trembling made that impossible. A violent shudder shook the boat from fore to aft. Shock after shock passed along the vessel's frame. Then the entire boat lurched starboard and came to a grinding, listing halt.

The *Rubi-Yacht* had run aground.

Corbin had forgotten to raise the centerboard!

"Dammit!" he moaned. "Why didn't I drag Medlow out of that boat?"

It was too late for that now.

Corbin sighed and began figuring out what to do.

chapter **eleven**

Corbin struggled to his feet and looked out across the bow. The shoreline lay less than thirty feet away. Only the sandy shoal separated his boat from the mica-glistening clays and the yellowish loam of the cove's western shore.

He held to the hatch and leaned out to see if he could assess the damage. A rust-colored sediment eddied in the water off starboard; the bow had beached itself on one of the shoal's gravelly spits in a seam of sandy orange mud.

It could have been worse, he thought.

Where should be begin? "Let's start in the galley," he said to himself.

Corbin ducked his head then stepped below. The boat was listing badly, but he could still stand in the galley's passageway. He leaned down and tried to crank the centerboard up, but the handle would not budge.

"Must be mired up to the hull," he mumbled.

Corbin surveyed the galley. Janet and Craig's picture listed with the boat. As he remembered it, he had fastened the frame onto a small metal plate which he had then bolted to the bulkhead. The picture had been slipped between the frame's glass and a cardboard backing. The picture would right itself with the boat.

What needed attention was the ice chest. Its lid had popped off and most of the ice had spilled out into the passageway. The dill pickle jar, chip bag, and potato salad carton had also fallen to the floor, but neither jar nor carton appeared damaged. Corbin picked them up first, along with the chips, and set them back in the ice chest. Then he began scooping up the ice with his hands until he had transferred most of it back into the chest. Finally, he replaced the lid.

He next retrieved the plastic water jug and set the athletic bag, for the second time, in the seat under the picture. The bag contained a change of clothing, several towels, and swimming suit, but there was no need to change his wet shorts or shirt now until he had examined the centerboard.

Corbin edged his way back out to the cockpit and climbed up onto the hatch. He held to the teakwood rails and pulled himself along, until he came to the shroud lines and the mast.

The boom had swung out starboard and was almost in the water. The headsail still lay in a collapsed white heap on the foredeck, its starboard sheet trailing in the water. Luckily, the knot in the end of the jib halyard had caught in the turning block at the top of the mast. He would have to shinny up the pole and haul it back down. Damn! The sun was very hot, and its glare off the hatch and on the water was merciless.

Corbin grabbed hold of the mast and, using it for support, sat down beside the gleaming pole and pulled the jib sheet out of the water. He then crawled across the Dacron sail and untied the anchor rope. Inching along the tilted deck, he dropped the anchor off portside. He felt the rope feed out about twelve feet altogether, then let out about another twenty feet or so. Corbin tied the rope tight about a cleat.

His deck shoes were slippery and still wet from his spill into the lake. Water oozed out of them with a forceful scrunch of his toes. The shoes will dry quickly enough, he thought, once the boat is freed.

He scooted back down to the mast, slipped off each shoe, laid each carefully on the jib, then peeled off his wet socks. He wrung them out and tossed them beside his shoes.

The bow appeared to be beached on about three feet of the sand bar. If he slipped off over the bow by the pulpit, he would easily mire in the spit's orange clay. He decided to inch toward midship and enter the water there.

He stood up, let go of the mast, stepped quickly toward starboard, and jumped in. Water gurgled up around his shorts and chest as his feet touched bottom in neck-deep water.

Corbin waited for the ocher sediment to settle before submerging and swimming toward the hull. He surfaced beside the boat for a big intake of air, then dove under the *Rubi-Yacht* and began groping with his hands along the hull.

He could feel the centerboard before he saw it. It loomed orange and hazy and longer than he knew it to be. He ran his fingers quickly down its leading edge until they stirred up more sediment. A foot or more of the board appeared to be wedged in the lake's mud. The mire felt soft enough, but a tremendous shove would be required to free the boat. The problem was finding the right fulcrum.

He returned to the surface for a second intake of air, then swam back under the hull toward the centerboard. This time he examined the keel and the centerboard slot. There was always the possibility that a root might have lodged in the slot, but he could feel none, nor was he aware of any stump residue on the bottom.

He examined the starboard side first, then swam under the hull to port. The board seemed solid enough, but until he could crank it back up, he could not determine what damage, if any, it had sustained.

He swam toward the anchor rope and began to pull himself up to portside. The world beneath the water seemed so quiet; everything suspended in primordial balance; at peace with itself, harmoniously fluid, yet timelessly at rest. He felt as if he had ventured into some ancient grotto, hallowed and set apart for the eternal journeyings of the gods.

As his face broke the surface, his mouth gulped for fresh air, and his nostrils inhaled the warmth that wafted gently across the lake. A web of wrinkles undulated in the water; a good stout wind was beginning to stir.

Corbin swam to the stern and pulled his way up the angled ladder. He climbed over into the cockpit and raised the lid to the sail locker.

"Where did I put it?" he wondered aloud, as he searched for an oar. He could see his inflatable dinghy, lying beneath the boom and tiller slipcovers. "But where is the oar?"

A nagging desperation nudged the edge of his consciousness, for he realized that, wherever the oar was, it would be too short to serve his needs. Would the gaff work? But he knew it was too limber. Then a third idea occurred to him.

Lowering the lid, Corbin made his way along the cockpit to the hatch; he stepped down into the galley and, supporting himself against the table, hurried toward the bulkhead. He ducked his head and entered the forecastle.

"Now where did we put it." he asked aloud. Then he remembered. He leaned forward, searched under the bunk to portside and found what he was searching for: a machete!

"Look, Dad! I'm a pirate!" Craig had said, whirling the big blade over his head.

"Well, don't cut yourself," Corbin had replied. "Bleeding pirates attract sharks."

"Oh, great, Dad! Nothing like a little confidence in your son!" Janet had frowned.

"OK, kid! Just don't bleed on the hatch."

"Sure, Dad! Watch!" Craig announced, as he swung the machete about in figure-eights, suddenly slashing the main canvas on the old *Wright Boat*.

Corbin pulled the machete out. It was rusted near the handle and all along the cutting edge. This will have to do, he thought. Corbin treaded his way back out to the cockpit and, holding the machete high above his head, jumped overboard again. He swam toward the shoal, waded across it, and swam on toward the clay embankment. He had to scale it on all fours—machete in hand—but he negotiated the head-high bluff easily enough, and, walking barefoot across the point's grassy slope, made his way gingerly toward a small copse of trees.

Mud and sweat covered his body; thousands of tiny mica specks, caught in the hair of his arms and legs, glistened as he stepped barefoot along. Corbin glanced down at his shirt and shorts. "They're ruined," he said. For they were as red as the ocher seam of mire and clay through which he had crawled.

When he arrived at the copse, he singled out a tall water oak—about four inches in diameter—and began cutting it down. The machete blade was brittle and dull, and Corbin did not want to snap or break it. He took short careful swings, just enough each time to take a good single bite of bark and wood out of the tree.

It took him five minutes to fell the sapling and another five or ten to hack the branches off its trunk. Corbin gripped the pole in both hands and tested it for balance. He estimated that it was about sixteen to eighteen feet long and weighed up to twenty pounds. He whacked off the leafy top of the young oak and began trimming the branch notches smooth.

Finally, he was satisfied.

Corbin was about to leave the copse when he spotted the *Columbia*, heeling its way smoothly out in the cove. Corbin instinctively reached for his hat to wave it, but brought, instead, his muddy hand, still clinching to the machete, down on his forehead. Fortunately, he did not cut himself, but he felt like a fool and felt an even deeper loss for the hat. "Dammit, Janet, I am sorry."

He watched the *Columbia* sail out into the lake and tack southward into the wind.

If only Jil might glance in his direction!

Surely she would turn back, if only she knew he was there!

"Jil, I need you!" he mumbled, gritting his teeth, as the *Columbia's* sails bore Jil farther and farther away.

She could not possibly see him or know it was he.

Corbin dragged the pole out of the copse and down to the bluff. While still standing on the clay escarpment, he lowered the pole onto the edge of the shore below and shinnied down it.

He waded out into the lake, balancing the pole in both hands, until the water grew chest-deep. Then he swam out to the shoal, pushing the pole in front of him, while clutching the machete in his right hand. He poled his way across the orange mire and swam on toward the stern of his boat.

Corbin rested momentarily beside the transom before wobbling the pole into the cockpit. Slowly, he climbed aboard. He placed the machete on the starboard cockpit seat and made his way toward the bow. He was careful not to snag the main halyard but did slip against the mast himself.

Straddling the jib, Corbin stepped cautiously up to the pulpit and, lowering the pole into the water, leaned into it with all his might. But the pole only sank in the mud.

Corbin pulled the pole up and tapped along the edge of the bottom for a firmer hold. He found one and bore down again with all his strength. His taut body stiffened but that was all. He kept bearing down on the pole until he felt the boat move ever so slightly. He bore down a third, fourth, and fifth time, each time feeling the boat slip a little more away from the bar. He could see the black crease in the ocher mud that the keel had made in the clay. Reaching his hands high up on the pole, he pulled down a sixth, seventh, and eighth time. Finally, the boat sucked free, with a sharp clacking of the halyard against the mast and a loud slapping of water beneath the hull. The halyard cracked against the mast a second time as the boat righted itself and drifted free.

With the pole still leaning perpendicular in the

mud, Corbin hurried toward the hatch; he hopped down into the cockpit and, kneeling beside the galley entrance, began cranking up the centerboard. The crank responded smoothly as Corbin rotated the handle in a clockwise direction for twenty turns.

He climbed back topdeck to inspect the jib cloth. He set his shoes and socks on the hatch and meticulously untangled the sail. Then he pulled on his wet socks and shoes and glanced up at the turning block. He did not relish climbing the mast, but it was either that or sail without the jib. A feeling of dread slipped over him, but he struggled to his feet and, taking hold of the mast, began to shinny slowly up the aluminum pole.

Only once before had Corbin made such a repair. And that had been with Craig's help. Now he would have to do it alone. Damn, he didn't like it. But he shinnied on.

The boat swayed to starboard as Corbin wrapped his legs tightly about the mast and pulled himself upward. The climb passed slowly, and Corbin relied on the strength of his arms as much as any power in his legs.

Corbin could feel the boat turn slowly as the hull sloshed with each upward tug of his arms and legs. Perspiration ran off his head and trickled slick under his armpits. The blistering sun bore down fiercely, as if to test his mettle to the limit.

"Up!" he whispered to himself. "Up!" he repeated, as his fingers groped nervously for the spreaders. Then he clutched them with all his strength and, flopping his arms over them, pulled himself up to a sitting position, his legs straddling the mast and dangling over the spreader arms.

Corbin peered down. Below, the *Rubi-Yacht* appeared long and narrow, its mast swaying, first to starboard, then slowly back to port. The murky water off the shoal bobbed rusty and muddy, while the darker water of the lake rippled deep blue, with the sun sparkling on his sails.

Hot sweat burned the corners of Corbin's eyes. Wiping them dry with his balled up fists, he inched his wet fingers along the mast and, gripping it as securely as he could, drew his legs in, and stood, with each foot on a spreader arm. He hugged the mast and glanced up toward the turning block.

The knot was barely within reach. Extending his left arm toward it, while clasping to the mast with his sweating right arm, he leaned out and, with trembling fingers, caught the end of the halyard and pulled it quickly toward his teeth. Placing the knot in his mouth, he lowered his buttocks and sat again on the spreaders. He rested there a full ten minutes, with the halyard clinched between his teeth, before shinnying on down to the hatch.

His arms and legs glistened with sweat; his muscles trembled with convulsions of fatigue. Releasing a sigh, he lashed the halyard in place, pulled on it to test its hold, then collapsed on the foredeck and lay back on the jib.

"Ah, Wright! You did it! By damn, you did!" He smiled, then rolled slowly over, and sat up.

Now all that remained to be done was to weigh anchor, crank up the outboard, and motor far enough out into the lake to be able to hoist the sails safely.

"But first to get out of this mess!" Corbin said. "And take a dip. Then get a beer!" he added, as he wiped a sweaty wrist across his lips and down the edges of his dry, cracked mouth.

Corbin sighed and began to grope his way stern-ward. As he did, he clawed off his soiled shirt and descended once more into the galley. There he removed his shoes, socks, and shorts. He stepped back up to the cockpit and, without hesitation, mounted the port seat and jumped off into the blue water of the glistening lake. "Ah!" he moaned, as he lay back and floated beside the boat for several minutes. Then he submerged, swam under the hull, and, breaking surface near the transom, pulled himself up the ladder, and reentered the galley. He slipped off his briefs, unzipped the athletic bag, pulled out a towel, and dried himself off. After rummaging about in the bag, he removed a clean pair of tan shorts, white socks, a white knit shirt, and a pair of clean underwear. He dressed while standing in the companionway, but sat in the booth to pull on his socks.

Somewhere in the forecastle he knew he had a second pair of shoes, so he slipped past the forward bulkhead and began searching for them in the hanging locker. He found them under an old plastic raincoat. They reeked of mildew, but they would do until his wet pair could dry.

Finally, he returned to the cockpit and set about to weigh anchor and get under sail. He lowered the motor into the water, scrambled back to the foredeck to attend to the anchor, then settled down beside the transom. He started the outboard and motored slowly out into the lake.

Five minutes later, he cut off the motor, pulled the outboard up and onto its catch, cranked down the centerboard and hoisted the sails.

His compass needle indicated a south-to-southwest bearing—a course to which, if he could hold, would bring him leeward of Lunch Island in about an hour. He glanced at his watch; it would soon be four.

The big green round-topped island lay hunkered low on the glaring horizon. If his estimation was accurate, the island lay at least two miles on a bobbing bearing of about 225 degrees.

I might just anchor there he thought, and spend the night.

He held his face to the breeze and began to hum "A-roving, a-roving." Then he sang quietly:

> *"A-roving, a-roving, a-roving's been my ruling;*
> *Alas, my love, poor Janet, a-roving I must go.*
> *A-roving, a-roving, a-roving's now my ruling;*
> *Alas, O love, my Janet, a-roving must I go."*

chapter **twelve**

I t was 5:15 when Corbin dropped anchor off Lunch Island's leeward tip. It seemed now that he had been sailing all day without rest, and that, somewhere deep within, he was still clinging to the *Nightstar's* brass plate and clutching Janet's gown. "Corbin! Get hold of yourself! Get with it!" he muttered.

He watched the gray weight sink slowly in the blue water until the murky depths concealed its stock, flukes, arms and all. He estimated that he had anchored in about nine feet of water.

A shallow beach extended out from the island, forming an underwater shelf that descended sharply just beyond his bow. The beach itself lay a good fifty yards away. The orange shoreline glistened with clay deposits and silicates. Clumps of black driftwood had washed onto its narrow strand. A tough green Bermuda grass, tall russet sedges, and low-growing sumacs formed a tight mantle over the eastern end of the island.

The sun's glare reflected fiercely on the water when Corbin glanced directly west toward the sun. Patches of small cumulus clouds still drifted high across the sky. Occasionally, they blotted out the sun, but the clouds were too small to eclipse the orb's dazzling rays that burned through the soft edges of the clouds.

Corbin felt keenly thirsty; his lips were parched, and his face and arms felt wind-burned and dry. He removed the skipper's cap and wiped a dark band of perspiration from above each ear. The breeze felt good against the matted dampness of his hair.

Corbin secured the anchor rope and returned across the hatch to the cockpit. He dropped down and entered the galley. Looping the cap's band over its hook, he loosened the lid of the ice chest, and slipped out a cold can of Coke. He popped off its key and sat down in the booth and began taking long, gulping drafts. He leaned over toward the ice chest and helped himself to a beef stick. Its tangy smoky flavor and chewy meat pleased him immensely. He could have eaten the entire pack of six, but he knew that one was all he needed. He finished the Coke and dropped the can in the plastic bag beneath the sink.

It was hot, both outside and within the galley, and Corbin's shirt and waistband were damp with sweat. Trickles of perspiration had coursed down his back and now caused considerable itching and discomfort.

Corbin struggled out of the seat and decided to undress and go swimming. He set the athletic bag on the table and unzipped it. The trunks he had brought were wrinkled and faded, but he unwadded the light tan suit, slipped out of his clothing, and, resting against the counter, pulled on the trunks.

He stepped out of the galley, up onto the port bench, straddled the guardrail, and jumped, arms forward, into the water. His head did not submerge, but water splashed all up around his back and chest and into his face. It felt cool and soothing to his hot skin.

Corbin gave a scissors kick with his legs and, forming breaststrokes with his arms, began swimming slowly toward the beach. Rolling onto his back, he spread out his arms, and let his legs and feet float however they would. He had to tread, now and then, but he lay in that position for ten to twelve minutes, relaxing and treading water when he had to, as he floated in the bobbing waves between the *Rubi-Yacht* and the island's beach.

Suddenly, Corbin's feet began to drag bottom. He had drifted considerably toward the shore. Rolling back onto his stomach, he swam the remaining few yards to the beach.

A large quantity of driftwood had washed up onto

the narrow strand. Corbin picked his way through the debris where he waded ashore.

The yellowish-sienna clay was hard-packed, and he was able to walk along the beach without sinking in the mire. He was about to pick up a sturdy root for a cane when a movement several yards beyond him caught his attention.

A large black watersnake had looped itself about a piece of driftwood. Its forked tongue licked the air for scent. The snake's head was cocked eerily to one side. Suddenly, the big fat serpent uncoiled itself and slithered out into the water. Corbin watched it swim away in a wide zigzag pattern, keeping itself parallel to the beach. It disappeared behind a clay shoal.

Corbin bent down and picked up the root. It was caked red with dry mud and glistened with tiny mica particles. Corbin rinsed it off in the lake and began climbing the embankment. He beat the ground with the root as he stepped carefully onto the island's grassy plain.

The grass was dry and the soil was hard. A light breeze sighed in the sedges. Corbin could hear the lake lapping gently behind him where it washed ashore.

The sun broiled down hot on his chest and arms and he broke out in a heavy sweat. He brought his left hand up to his brow to ward off the sun's glare.

The island seemed so desolate, deserted, wild. He realized he had not visited it in years. Not since Craig's graduation from college.

Corbin walked on, poking in the grass with his "cane" and swatting occasionally at mosquitoes. Several feet ahead yawned the first of many shallow depressions. They were shallow craters, left behind from the practice bombing runs that dated back to World War II. Now they were overgrown with briars, grass, sumac bushes, and weeds. Near the edge of the depression, mangled flakes of bomb-casing lay rusting in the weeds.

Corbin could imagine the big old-style B–25 bombers lumbering noisily across the lake to drop their practice bombs over the island before banking in a glare of propeller blades and fuselage and winging their way back to Otis Airbase.

"War. The tatters of war. Even here," he whispered to himself. He wondered if Doolittle and his squadron had thought about Lunch Island as they dropped their bombs over Tokyo.

He had missed his generation's war. He had missed it by one year, having turned twenty-six in '64. By then he and Slaygard had launched their own firm. And he, Janet, and Craig had moved out to York Drive. To the suburbia of the sixties. In a time and place thousands of miles away from the bombing runs of Vietnam.

Corbin stared down into the gravel-bottomed pit. Aiken's son had not been so fortunate. That was a part of Aiken's life he had learned of only within the past few years.

He knew that Jil was Aiken's second wife and considerably younger than Aiken. But he never knew the circumstances of his first marriage, or why it had failed, or of any other children it might have spawned.

It was a late July afternoon, just before closing. Corbin had escorted his secretary to the door and was about to lock it, when Aiken stepped off the elevator.

"Wait! Please!" called his big friend. There was a disturbed expression in Aiken's eyes. A sadness possessed him in a way that Corbin had never seen. "Are you alone?" he asked.

"Yes. Totally at your disposal," he replied.

"Good! I need to see you in private. I want you to hear something. And keep it for me," he mumbled. "You do have a tape recorder, or player, I mean?"

"Sure. Several. What size do you need?"

"For a quarter-inch reel," he said. "You must hear this," he repeated, with an urgency that Corbin had never observed in his broker friend before.

"This way," Corbin said, as he led Aiken back to

his office and to a storage cabinet. "There's a player right here. Somewhere in this cabinet, I know."

Aiken was silent and had taken a seat.

Corbin opened the cabinet and dragged out a rather large recorder. He carried it to his desk and swung it up onto a pile of documents and correspondence clutter. "You'll pardon this mess," he muttered, but Aiken's mind seemed miles away when Corbin turned to look at him.

"Sure!" Aiken finally managed to reply, as he reached inside his suit pocket and produced a small reel and crinkled envelope. "I hate to burden Jil with it. But I must keep it somewhere. Outside of Jil, you're the only one I trust, the only one I know who will understand," he said.

"I'm listening," Corbin replied. "Please, go on," he said, as he unwound the player's cord and plugged it into a wall socket. Then he sat on the edge of the desk, opposite Aiken.

Aiken handed Corbin the reel and began fumbling with the envelope. He slipped out a crumpled letter and what appeared to be a map.

"Corbin, this will be just between the two of us," Aiken reiterated. A tight sigh slipped faintly from the older man's lips. "This is a letter," he explained, "and a map from a guy who was in Tom's flight-mission the day his plane went down over North

Vietnam.

"I've never talked about this before, but I had a son who was killed there. His plane went down ten years ago this month. They still list him as 'missing in action,' but I know better. He's dead and God only knows where his remains were tossed. This letter is from a navigator who roomed with Tom and who recorded the mission. Something they were required to do, he says. It has Tom's voice on it," he murmured.

"This buddy felt that I ought to have the tape. Or at least a copy of it. In any event, he's sent it to me," Aiken sighed. "Along with a map, pinpointing the area of their mission, and a letter explaining some of the terms they use. Like 'Ethan Charlie'—U.S. radar out over the Gulf of Tonkin, he says—and other jargon and call signals."

He handed the letter and map to Corbin. "I want to hear it one more time," he said, whispering the words. "I want you to hear it with me. Then I want you to keep it here. Where only the two of us know where it is."

There were tears now in Aiken's eyes, which the big man rubbed at softly.

"I understand," Corbin said. "You and I will be the only ones to know."

Corbin glanced over the letter and looked at the map. The map showed an area of Thailand, Laos,

Cambodia, and mostly North Vietnam. Hanoi was circled; a ridge of mountains to the north of it was labeled "Thud Ridge." The Gulf of Tonkin was also identified. A red *X* had been penciled in on the southern edge of the ridge.

Corbin threaded the reel onto the player and turned on the machine.

A crackling drone invaded the silence of the office. The navigator's breathing rasped calmly amid the radio's static.

"The missile's getting noisy," he said to the pilot. "Can you turn it down!"

"How's that? Any better?"

"Roger!"

The quiet breathing resumed.

"Got a one-ring SAM radar out about one o'clock."

"OK. Take a doppler fix on our position," the pilot requested.

"Twenty-one, zero-five-north. One-zero-four, fifty six-west," the navigator recited, as he read back their coordinates.

"Ethan Charlie here. We've got you on radar. Can you read me, Bobcat?"

"Roger," someone replied.

"Ethan Charlie to Bobcat. Squawk flash, please."

"Roger. This is Bobcat." It was the strike force commander's voice.

"I've got triple-A guns in the target area," reported the navigator to the pilot.

"Beaver has guns in the target area," the pilot repeated. "This is Beaver leader to flight units. We've got guns in the target area."

"Roger," a voice affirmed.

"Guns no threat," said the navigator. "They're out about one-thirty."

"Ethan Charlie to Bobcat. You have bandits at two-thirty. Thirty-five miles out. Closing."

The pilot's breathing quickened and deepened in tone. "Beaver leader to flight. Afterburners! Now!" he ordered.

"One-ring SAM radar about one-thirty. No threat," the navigator reported. "Disregard your activity light. Repeat, no threat."

"All righty!" sighed the pilot. "But keep your eye on our tail."

"Got a one-ring SAM at one-thirty. No threat," the navigator once again assured the pilot.

"Beaver's got numerous fire cans out of Viet Tri," the pilot radioed his flight unit. "Put the doppler on the peak," he ordered the navigator.

"Fire cans and SAMs out of the target area," droned the navigator. His voice was calm and unhurried. "Again, no threat."

"No threat," the pilot repeated, relieved.

Static hummed steadily in the background.

"Beaver leader! Beaver leader to number two. I've got two bandits coming at you at two o'clock."

"Roger." It was Tom's voice.

"Where the fuck did they go?" blurted Beaver leader.

"I've got them at one o'clock," replied the navigator.

"Holy shit! There they are! One! Two! Three! I've got *five* bandits coming at you, number two!" shouted Beaver leader. "Clean 'em up! Now!" he ordered.

"Look at those suckers go!" Tom said. "I see your tanks dropping. Along with the lady fingers," his voice popped erratically over the radio.

Increased static and inhaling and exhaling rasped heavily against the background hum.

"Where's our CAP?" asked Beaver leader. "Is the CAP up there?"

"Roger. Got 'em at nine o'clock high," said the navigator.

There was more static, a screech, and increased labored breathing.

"They're gone! The MIGS are gone!" exclaimed the pilot. "Let's go back and do our job."

"Two more coming in low," said the navigator.

"Break! Break right!" called Beaver leader. "Dammmnnn! They've gone on by!"

"They're coming through the strike force," warned Tom. "They're passing through now!"

"Someone's going down!" a new voice interjected. His breathing was very heavy.

A sharp, crackling drone drowned out Tom's reply. A deep, beeping tone erupted in the background.

"SAMs! One o'clock! Two rings!" the navigator suddenly interrupted. "No threat!" he called out, relieved.

"God! They look like telephone poles!" observed the pilot.

"Yeah!" the navigator replied.

"Bobcat to Beaver leader! Bobcat to Beaver leader!" It was the strike-force commander's voice. "Bobcat lead is on the target area. Short! I'm short! A mile short!" he called back.

"SAMs coming in at two o'clock!" an excited, unidentified voice interrupted.

"Take a dive! Take a dive!" a third voice warned.

"Your bombs! You've still got your bombs!" blurted the third voice.

"Bear Lodge to Beaver leader. Come in."

"Beaver leader here. I read you," the pilot said.

"You've got one going down. The canopy's off."

"Roger! Who is it?" he asked.

"Can't tell," said the navigator.

A beeping, warning tone whined noisily amid the

drone.

"Dammit!" cursed the pilot. "It's Tom! They've got Tom."

There was a long silence, amid the heavy breathing of both the pilot and the navigator.

"Beaver leader! I've got his chute over Thud Ridge," called in the third voice.

"See him!" Beaver leader replied. "I see him."

A crackling drone broke the tension of the moment, then a voice. "I'm down!" It was Tom's. "There's a lot of traffic down here. It's coming up fast."

"Try to find a place to hide," urged the pilot. "We'll call the Sandies in. OK?"

"They're shooting wildly!" Tom radioed. "This is Blue-three. Blue-three!"

The navigator's breathing drowned out Tom's emission.

"Yes, Blue-three! Come in!" said the pilot.

"Blue-three! This is Blue-three! O God! I . . ."

An abrupt drone hummed amidst the background chatter on the radio.

"Head down the ridge! I'll see if I can spot him on the ground," said the navigator.

More heavy breathing.

"He must be in the trees," said the navigator.

"He doesn't reply on the radio," said Beaver leader.

"Put the doppler on the turning point," he added to the navigator.

"Bear Lodge to Beaver leader. Bear Lodge on bingo fuel. Outbound! Over."

"Roger, Bear Lodge. Beaver leader on bingo, too. Heading for the tanks," he said, as the crackling emissions weakened, the drone hummed low, and the tape suddenly clicked off.

"Just like that!" Aiken exclaimed. "Ah, Tom!" the big man moaned, as he raised his hands to his face and emitted a faint sob. Then he began to cry profusely, as Corbin slipped to his side and put his arm around his friend's shoulders and sought to comfort him.

chapter **thirteen**

"**A**hoy, sailor! Ahoy!" a voice interrupted Corbin's daydream.

He turned in the direction of the voice and stared out toward his boat. A sleek craft had dropped sails and was gliding past the *Rubi-Yacht*. It cleared his boat and drifted slightly closer into shore. Its skipper had clambered forward and was casting the boat's anchor off the starboard bow. Corbin's eyes caught the flash of the sun as it gleamed against the anchor's flukes, just before the weight splashed into the lake.

It was Jil.

Corbin retraced his steps through the grass, scrambled down the embankment to the beach, and waded out waist-deep into the water.

"What are you doing out here?" Jil called.

Corbin could see the smile on her face as well as sense her excitement and surprise.

"Are you all right?"

"Of course!" he yelled. He had longed for this

121

moment. He cast his cane aside, dove into the water, and began swimming toward the *Columbia.* As he rotated his face sideways out of the water and brought each arm alternately forward in the crawl stroke, he could see the sun glint golden off the rumpled jib behind Jil. Her face and hair glowed amber in the sun's late afternoon hue;so also did her white blouse and shorts.

The effect of the sunlight on her bronze silhouette heightened Corbin's emotions, and, as he swam toward her, he hated to put his face back into the water. Two, three, four more strokes, and you will be there, he told himself.

He brought his legs forward and began to tread water. "I am so glad you stopped. Won't you join me for a swim?" he smiled, as he drifted toward the hull and rested against it.

Jil had seated herself on the collapsed jib and was holding to the jib stay with her left hand. Her legs were tan and her thighs rounded and smooth. The curves of her breasts were quite noticeable where they pressed against her blouse. Her reddish-blonde hair twitched carelessly in the light breeze. He was embarrassed to stare at her and was still sorting through his reverie of Tom and Aiken. But he realized how deeply he loved her and how much he wanted her and needed her.

"Corbin, that's the nicest offer I've had all day," she smiled. "If you'll give me just a minute, I'll change and be right with you."

"I'll wait for you by the transom," he said.

Corbin watched her pull herself up and thread her way past the shroud lines and mast. As she scooted across the hatch and down into the cockpit, he swam parallel to the boat and groped his way toward the stern.

The water felt only moderately cool. Corbin realized that the lake's surface temperature was easily in the mid-to-upper eighties.

"Must be in the nineties," he called, as he bobbed in the water beside the transom.

"As of an hour ago, it was ninety-four," Jil replied. "I feel so hot and grimy."

"You'll enjoy the swim."

Corbin held to the stern and treaded water slowly. Other than their two boats, all he could see were the low incoming waves, a bluish-slate, and gently rolling.

"There!" she said.

Corbin looked up. She was wearing a black single-piece stretch bathing suit that fit her waist and hips snugly and cupped her breasts only sparsely. Two narrow black shoulder straps drew the suit securely against her body.

He grasped the ladder's right rail and held his left hand up to Jil as she descended the rungs. She took his hand and slipped into the water. Then he guided her away from the transom and the rolling of the *Columbia*. He let go and began pulling away slowly in a light backstroke as she swam toward him on her side.

"Oh, this is marvelous!" she said. "Another hour and I would have had to jump overboard."

"I'm glad you waited," he said.

"Me too," she replied.

They swam away from the *Columbia* and its bow.

"Corbin, why do you always make me feel so human? I suppose you know you do?" She began to tread water and drift toward him.

Corbin brought his arms in and swam slowly toward her. "Don't say anything," he said, as he leaned toward her and kissed her lips.

Tears glistened in her eyes, but she remained bobbing in the water and returned his kiss with a firm open-mouthed kiss of her own. "I just want to swim with you beside me," she said.

He clasped her hand and pulled her along, and the two of them swam slowly together, away from the *Columbia* and parallel with the island. They swam like that for ten to fifteen minutes, with the waves rolling gently past them and sometimes bobbing them momentarily until a succeeding swell rolled in.

"Let's swim ashore and rest for a moment," she suggested. "Or walk along the beach."

"Here." He took her by the hand again and drew her along, until they were in water shallow enough to allow them to wade to the beach.

They sloshed ashore where the strand was very narrow and the silicates in the clay glistened yellowish amidst the shattered fragments of gleaming quartz. Corbin stepped in front of her as they ambled along, lest a second snake should slither out from the driftwood and frighten her.

"This island has always fascinated me," she said. "Aiken and I used to visit it frequently when we were first married. Then Aiken lost interest, or preferred to visit it alone. But I can understand why.

"You know, Corby, Aiken lost a son in Vietnam. Missing in action, they told him. Aiken could never talk about it to me, but he could come here, by himself, and be alone with his son."

"It is a beautiful island."

"But it is so lonely. So quiet."

"Maybe that's part of its beauty. Listen to the quiet," he said. "You can hear the breeze and the wind and the lake lapping against the shore. Or the distant drone of a motor. Otherwise, it's just yourself and silence."

They stopped and together listened to the sound of the breeze in the dry grass behind them and to the lake's incessant sighing where the water washed ashore along the island.

"It is even more beautiful in the fall," Corbin said, "when the hardwoods have deepened in color. You can pick out the red maples from the muted purples of the gums and the yellow of the poplars, even from this distance across the lake."

"Don't you ever get lonely when you come here?" Jil asked. "It's the loneliness and the silence that's so hard for me, now that Aiken's . . . 'dead.' It's just like he's dead!" she blurted. "O God, it would be better if he were!"

Corbin put his arm around her shoulder and held her tightly against his chest.

"That's a horrible thing to say, isn't it? Or even to think! To wish someone you've lived with for fifteen years were dead."

"No, it isn't," Corbin said. "It's being honest; it's being true, however much it hurts. Don't you realize that I was beginning to feel like that when Janet was dying and you'd come around? Don't you realize I love you and want you as much as I wanted Janet, even when she was alive and well?"

He kissed her eyes and felt for her lips with his mouth. She put her hands around his shoulders and pressed her lips to his.

"Please take me back to the *Columbia!*" she said, whispering the words in his ear.

"I don't want you to leave now. Please!" he said.

"Who said I was going to leave?" She took his hand and began to draw him back into the water.

He followed her movements with his eyes and waded into the water with her. There was a glow about her face, as well as a tenderness and a sorrow that nudged him deeply.

"Dammit, Jil," he whispered, "I mean no wrong, but I love you."

"And I you," she said, as she leaned into the water and began swimming toward her yacht.

Corbin sank into an oncoming wake and swam silently beside her, out toward the *Columbia*. He helped her climb the ladder and smiled when she pressed his hand and looked deeply into his eyes. He followed her across the cockpit, into the galley, and entered the forecastle with her. There he drew her whole body against his as she slipped off her straps and he tugged at his own shorts. Then he lay his face in her breasts and kissed her and lay down with her on the V-bunk and made love to her amidst her kisses. He caught her tears with his thumbs and kissed them away.

For a long while he lay there, he in her arms, and

she in his, and neither said anything to the other.

"I need to get up," she finally said.

"I hate to let you go."

"I'll still be right here, in the forecastle."
"OK," he said and kissed her as she slipped out of the bunk and partially covered herself with her swimming suit.

"I need to wash and get dressed."

"I should do the same," he said.

"What time is it?"

"Almost seven."

"I need to leave, Corbin. It'll take me at least an hour or more to get back to the marina."

"That'll put you in at dark," he said. "Please don't go. Stay here with me. I plan to stay here for the night."

She turned and looked at him somewhat bemused and yet nonplused. "Are you serious?"

"Uh-huh! I really do. And I can offer you dinner, too. An evening out on the lake. With a drink and a four-course meal. Sound tempting?"

"Sounds crazy, but I like it." She returned to the bunk and bent down and kissed him.

He slipped his arm around her bare waist and drew her back onto the bunk.

"Corbin!" she objected. "Please, I need to wash. And so do you."

Nevertheless he kissed her and lay against her while once again she received his arms and body.

"You are wonderful," she said. "I haven't been so happy in years."

"You are what is wonderful. God forgive me, but as much as I loved Janet, I fell in love with you that day we had lunch with you and Aiken in Ballentine. Remember?"

"Do I remember? Your eyes looked like a puppy's searching for milk. You should be ashamed."

"I was and still am. For I deeply loved, and will always love, Janet. But now there's only you. And I love you, and can't feel guilty for that. In spite of Janet or Aiken."

"What are we going to do? I just can't up and divorce Aiken, as if he never mattered, or were some lifeless piece of tissue!"

"I don't know," Corbin said. "But we will think of something. We will manage it somehow."

"Will you please let me up, now!" she said as she kissed him.

"Of course," he returned her kiss.

Corbin watched Jil from the bunk while she washed herself in the galley sink. There was such an innocence and loveliness about her, though what they had just done was clearly adulterous. He sat up and rubbed his face in his hands and leaned out and kissed her.

"Please don't make me feel any worse than I do," Jil said. "You are so persistent."

"I can't help it." He kissed her on the chin.

"Maybe we can see each other quietly, until Aiken's condition changes," she suggested.

"Let's not try to plan it," he whispered. "Let's just accept it, until we can manage it, somehow," he hesitated, "honorably. I don't want to hurt Aiken any more than you do, and I certainly don't want to hurt you. Or give the Columbia gossip mills anything more to devour."

"I know it's wrong, Corby. But deep in my heart, I want to believe that what we've done is right."

She began drying herself with a towel and redressing.

"I'm sorry if I came across so eager," he said.

"I understand," she leaned down and kissed him. "There's no need to apologize. Come on and wash and get dressed," she handed him the towel. "I'm famished and ready for that four-course meal."

"I'll need to swim over to get things ready. Then put your fenders down and I'll motor over and we'll raft the boats together for the night."

She shook her head, still bemused at him, but smiled and kissed him as he wriggled past her into the galley.

chapter **fourteen**

It was past seven-thirty before Corbin emerged from the *Rubi-Yacht's* galley. He wore the tan shorts and white knit shirt he had donned earlier. He had slipped back into his deck shoes which, by now, had dried hard. In an hour or two, though, he knew they would supple up again.

The *Columbia* rode quietly at anchor less than thirty feet to port. Jil had lowered her fenders and had retired to the galley. Corbin assumed she was dressing or resting in the forecastle.

A light breeze jangled the halyards and jerked whimsically at the telltale ribbons. The sun had settled low and rouge behind a lumbering gray cloud that seemed to squat heavily on the horizon. The orb's golden rays illuminated the convoluted folds of the cloud's western edge.

All across the southeastern sky the clouds had thickened, and still farther south-to-southeast, a range of thunderheads towered in awesome splendor.

Corbin hesitated at the galley entrance, stepped back inside, and flipped on the radio.

"Current temperatures remain in the nineties. Ninety-two in the midlands; ninety in the upstate. Expected lows tonight in the mid-to-upper eighties. Thundershowers should pass through the state this evening.

"A storm watch remains in effect for most of Florida and the coast of Georgia. Gale winds have risen to fifty knots. The tropical storm is expected to move off the Atlantic coast during the night.

"Tomorrow's highs should range in the mid-nineties. Sixty-percent chance of rain in the morning; clearing to moderate conditions by late afternoon."

Corbin flipped off the switch and stepped back out into the cockpit. The *Columbia's* mast, shrouds, and stays formed a starkly etched silhouette against the distant pink thunderheads to the south. I need to help her furl her mainsail and stow the jib, he thought.

He climbed up on the hatch and, with his left foot, nudged the port side's two fenders over the decktracks along the hull. While near the pulpit, he weighed anchor and laid it forward along the bow.

He retraced his steps to the cockpit, hopped down, and leaned out over the stern. He lowered the outboard in the water, started the motor, put it in reverse, and backed the *Rubi-Yacht* slowly away from its point of anchorage. Pulling the tiller in, he forced the bobbing boat southward, and worked the craft slowly in the *Columbia's* direction. He cut the motor, pushed the tiller starboard, and let the boat drift closer and closer up against Jil's vessel. Then he hurried forward and dropped the anchor off his starboard bow.

The two boats bumped gently together and drifted apart again by several feet. Corbin returned to the cockpit, opened the sail locker, and fetched a spare length of line. He tied one end about his port winch and looped the soft pliable cord about the *Columbia's* opposite winch. He pulled gently on the rope, slowly drawing the two boats together. He dropped a second loop about the *Columbia's* winch and tied off the rope around a nearby cleat. The sterns now drifted about a foot apart. The anchors would hold the bows close enough, he reasoned.

He had tied the boats together while in a seated position and wondered why Jil had not come out to help him. Rising, he descended into the galley again to retrieve his ice chest and assemble the necessary paper cups, plates, and plastic utensils they would need.

He glanced at Janet and Craig's photo on the bulkhead wall, overlooking the booth. "I love you," he whispered to them. "And I know you love me."

Then he turned, and, gathering the food items in his arms, struggled out of the galley for Jil's boat.

As he stepped aboard her yacht, he realized she had turned on the cabin's lights and had set her own booth's table with napkins, fancy paper plates and even wine glasses. The aroma of steamed vegetables and savory sauce of a faintly spicy nature aroused a hunger he had not experienced since Janet's death.

"Hey, what is this!" he called, as he stumbled eagerly into the galley, balancing his Styrofoam ice chest and picnic cutlery in his arms.

"It's our dinner," she said. "I don't trust your 'four-course meal.' "

"Well, I'm not so sure I do either, but I didn't expect this."

"You're still on for the dinner, but let's do that another time."

"Where did you get all this?" he nodded toward the stove, as he set his ice chest on the counter beside the gas range.

"Aiken never liked to eat sandwiches more than once a day. We've always kept a well-supplied larder aboard." She raised the lid on the food locker beneath the forward seat in the booth. "Behold! Everything but canned goose and caviar. And sardines!" she added. "The smell makes me sick."

Corbin bent down and studied the locker's contents. Cans of tuna, spaghetti, soup, complete Chinese meals, dry noodles, and packages of rice, grits, cereal, coffee, and melba toast lined the locker. And rolled in paper towels for protection lay three bottles of uncorked wine. Corbin slipped one out of its paper. "B&G Chardonnay!" he read. "What's on the stove?" he asked.

"Sweet and sour pork and mixed oriental vegetables."

Corbin shook his head in amazement. "I guess we can tough it out with this," he grinned.

"The opener's down there somewhere," she said.

He found it, then stood and bent down to kiss her.

She kissed him and put her hands around his neck and kissed him again. "I wouldn't do this for anyone but you. Open the wine now and leave me alone for a second."

He kissed her and stepped out into the cockpit. He carried the Chardonnay in one hand and juggled the wine opener in the other. He sat down on the port bench and watched her through the galley entrance. Tears were glistening in her eyes.

"Just open the damn bottle!" she said. "And let me cry in peace. Can't you see I love you?"

"Just don't dilute the gravy," he said, as he screwed the skewer into the bottle's cork and pulled up on the cork.

"It's ready," she said.

Corbin brought the wine in and set it on the table. Jil had served his plate and was in the process of serving her own.

Corbin uncorked the bottle and poured each of them a glass. The clear pale yellowish wine gurgled noisily out of the bottle's neck and sparkled honey-like in each glass.

"To thee," he said, as he raised his glass and clinked it against hers.

Corbin sniffed its fruity bouquet and sipped the first gulp of warm wine, relishing its tart alcoholic taste. Then he took a second drink and set the glass beside his plate.

They sat opposite each other in the booth. Corbin could not help but smile when he glanced across the table at Jil and at her gently rounded breasts beneath her blouse.

"How I love you!" he said. "Let me count the ways," he smiled, as he looked intently at each breast.

"You are a rake!" she laughed. "But I love you."

"Your cuisine is quite good.

"Would that it were mine! But you will have to praise Master La Choy and his boys," she smiled.

"*Alors!* To the hoi polloi of La Choy!" he addressed his plate. "And to your eyes and breasts."

"Are you always such a devil?"

"Only because you make me joyful," he said.

"Have you always been this crazy? Or is it me?" she laughed.

"It is truly thee," he said, as he stuffed a forkful of sweet and sour pork into his mouth. "Truly thee, and thee alone. Canst thou not tell?"

"I see! Kiss me!" she whispered. "And stop mumbling in that medieval shit." Her face glowed with happiness as she leaned across the table.

"Ah!" he laughed. "Now, sweet wench, what hast thou for dessert?"

"Wench? How your appetites soar! Knave! You have had your dessert!"

"Fruit in its season! *C'etait très délicieux.* Are there seconds?"

"Maybe," she smiled.

"C'est bon!" he grinned. "Damn! But you are the finest thing that has befallen me in years." He stood up and leaned across the table and kissed her again.

"Why don't you see about your boat and furl our sails for us, while I clean up. Incidentally, what was the 'four-course-meal'?"

Corbin glanced at her and smiled. He turned toward the ice chest and popped off its lid. "A cold beer . . ."

"I might could use that later," she interrupted him.

"Beef sticks!" He held them up. "Corn chips. Ham

and cheese sandwiches. And potato salad," he winced, as he held up the clear, plastic carton of greenish-gray salad.

"Ugh! And you were serious about that! Corbin, how awful!" she laughed. "Poor man! We have got to alter your diet, before you die on that stuff."

"I agree."

Corbin pressed the cork down tightly on the wine bottle and placed it in the ice chest. Most of the ice had melted, but the water ached his hand, it was so cold. He set the lid back on, kissed Jil, and squeezed out the galley to the cockpit.

It took Corbin twenty minutes or more to fold up both jibs, replace each in its sailbag, and snap the mainsail covers on both booms. He then turned on each boat's mast lights and pulled up his outboard motor as well as Jil's. All was ready for the night.

Corbin glanced at his watch. It was close to nine.

The sun had set, but the western horizon, over the island, still retained a reddish glow. Far off to the south, the thunderheads had continued to build and had formed a large stalled storm system. Stars were faintly visible overhead, but the highest reaches of the storm cloud reflected the ashen-pink rays of the long-since departed sun. Pale shimmers of lightning glowed within the huge cloud, sometimes appearing pink and sometimes a blushed-gold. "Come here, Jil," Corbin said, as he stood outside the *Columbia's* galley. "Come, and see this."

Jil poked her head out of the galley and held her hand up for Corbin to take. The two seated themselves on the starboard bench and watched the lightning as it flashed silently in the cloud.

They sat for a long while together, facing the slowly darkening cloud, and enjoyed the breeze and listened to the boats, as the two bobbing vessels slapped water off of each other's hull.

"How did you meet Aiken?" Corbin asked Jil. "If I may know? I've always wondered that."

"It's a long story." She pressed both her hands around his right hand and held it between her thighs.

"I have all night," he said.

Her eyes sparkled in the cabin's light as she turned to him. "Do you really want to know?"

"Some of it," he said. "But nothing you wouldn't want to share. Or that's none of my business."

"His first wife died in an automobile wreck. It was a single-car accident, he said. I never pressed him for more. All I know is that he had just lost a son, still listed as missing in action, and now a wife, and that he was lonely and searching for companionship and love."

"Sounds like me."

"No. You're quite different," she smiled. "Aiken's love was always awkward, aloof, almost cold."

"You don't have to tell me this," he said.

"I wanted you to know. That's all. Whatever you and I have, is wonderfully different."

He put his hand on her thigh and rubbed it gently.

"I want to go on," she kissed him. "I wasn't exactly any prize, myself." She held her head back and let the breeze tug at her hair.

"I was twenty-eight when I met him. It was at a party in a motel. He was representing my mother's estate, and I was there as her heir, and a number of investment people from Atlanta were there, trying to lure new clients. After their initial presentations, Aiken took me aside and recommended we keep out. We talked for a long time," her voice trembled, sliding off into silence. "One thing led to another. He invited me out to dinner. We went to bed. I had gotten loused up on drugs—back in the sixties, after dropping out of Emory—and here was a man, even if he was thirteen years older, who cared and whose company made me feel wanted, if not loved. So when he proposed, I accepted."

"I love you," Corbin said. "My life has been singularly uncomplicated, until you."

A sly look of incredulity stole across her face. "Uncomplicated?" she repeated. "Janet always struck me as being very *complicated*. Reading philosophy and all. Is that not true?"

"Yes. I suppose so. I always thought of that aspect as just part of her father's influence. He was the *crazy* one, if you think I'm bad. She was very attached to him, and after his death became moody and withdrawn. But it was a moodiness I could respect. A part of her I never had trouble loving. It just deepened her as a mystery I was fated to love."

"I don't think I was ever fated for anything. I've just bumped along and accepted life as it is. Until Aiken's stroke. And now."

They sat together in silence, listening to the lake's waves slosh against the two hulls.

"Jil, I want you to marry me. I want you to be patient with me. I don't want to offend you, or wound Aiken any more than one has to. But there are legal ways we can . . ."

"Please, Corbin! Let's not think of that now. Let's just enjoy this together, and think about that later. I've got to visit Aiken tomorrow. I've got to drive to Florence and sit by his side. I have to be his wife, no matter how much it hurts you or me. You have to be patient with me. At least until I see how things develop and can sort out what I need to do. Kiss me, now," she said. "Make me feel human! Help me feel clean and whole in my mind! The way I feel clean and whole in my heart."

Corbin put his arm around her waist and kissed her ear and temple and the hair above her ear. He regretted the pressure he had put on her and knew he had to hold off.

"Love is strange," he said. "It's an affirmation I never thought I'd get a second chance to make.

"Once when God Boy—you know who God Boy was?"

"Oh, yes!" she laughed. "Janet frequently called him that."

"Well, once when God Boy and I were passing through Cleveland, we arrived at an intersection at the same time a Jewish funeral procession was passing by. By chance, a wedding party was coming down the street, in the opposite direction. The car all decorated and everything! The horn blaring, cans rattling. I glanced toward the people in the funeral cars, expecting to find grimaces of anger and annoyance, but instead saw smiles of approval. They began waving to the kids in the car. The funeral procession stopped. They yielded to the wedding party. I've never been able to forget that. I can still see it now, as if it were still taking place. They stopped and waved to those kids in the car."

Tears had gathered in Jil's eyes and began to run freely down her cheeks. "Corbin! Please hold me, tight! Just hold me as tight as you can," she said. So he held her and absorbed her body's quivering with the closeness of his chest and arms.

They talked some more. About the things they liked to do, visit, eat, drink. It was close to eleven, and the stars overhead were especially bright.

A motorboat passed somewhere off stern. They could hear its low gurgling in the water long before they saw its stern light.

"I think it's the lake patrol," Corbin said. "But I can't tell. It could be fishermen."

"Let's go to bed," Jil said. "I am absolutely dead, emotionally and physically. You will be a good boy," she said. "You don't snore?"

"I hope not," he smiled. "And I will be a good boy. For a while."

"For at least eight hours, I hope. Come on. I'll help you make the bed. Let's sleep in the berth in the galley. It's so much more comfortable than the bunk in the forecastle."

"OK. I'll follow you."

They descended to the galley, collapsed the dinette table, and converted the booth into a double bed. Jil brought some sheets out of the locker in the forecastle, and the two of them spread them across the booth's cushions.

Corbin turned off the cabin's lights, and slipped off his shorts. He could hear Jil slipping out of her shorts and blouse. He removed his shirt.

She got in bed first and scooted across the cushions. He lay down beside her and put his arm around her as she pulled up the sheet.

He became alive again sexually as he lay next to her, but he did not want to force himself on her. She rolled toward him and put her hands on him. He buried his face against her bosom, and they made love again in the silence of the cabin, with only the sound of the breeze rattling the cables and the noise of the waves sloshing against the hulls to distract them, and later to lull them to sleep.

chapter **fifteen**

Corbin awoke abruptly from a sound sleep. Jil's back lay against his chest; his left arm lay draped about her waist. The sheet had been kicked aside and lay rumpled about their hips. He could hear Jil breathing: rhythmic, light, serene. But he could not see her. Darkness smothered all light in the cabin. He felt clammy, hot.

He caught his breath and wondered why he had awakened. He heard the wind moaning past the rigging and sighing against the mast. The wires jingled as the boat rocked and dipped and rubbed against the *Rubi-Yacht*. He could hear the vinyl fenders squeaking and waves slapping between the two craft.

The wind was up.

Corbin raised his arm ever so lightly from Jil's waist, and slid silently out of the berth. He rose quietly in the dark hush of the galley and crept toward the cockpit. He did not want to rouse Jil, nor frighten her if she should awaken in the dark. He stole toward the exit and climbed up the step and out into the cockpit.

All across the south, the night loomed black, starless, windy. The distant glow of Columbia created a haunting mist that hovered in the east. The air felt cool and moist with impending rain.

Corbin glanced at his watch; it was 2 *a.m.* He looked across the *Rubi-Yacht* to the north, to the northwest, and to the northeast. There the sky scintillated in a sheen of blinking stars. They were everywhere, filling the night like bright white coals.

High in the northwest sky tilted the brilliant outline of the Northern Cross. Its five luminous points pulsated majestically amidst the silent spaces of the night. The Big Dipper's handle had sunk below the horizon, but the lip of its lambent cup still pointed unwaveringly toward the North Star.

"Always sight her first," God Boy had taught him. "And look for Cassiopeia. And when you've spotted her, you'll know where you are."

"I see her now," whispered Corbin, as he searched the sky above the North Star, where the great constellation loomed like a lazy W or a child's wobbly M. "Cassiopeia, sitting in her chair, keeing an eye on Cepheus," he whispered to himself.

To the east, his eyes made out the dim cluster of the Pleiades and Perseus, lying in the arc between the

Seven Sisters. "Perseus, savior of Andromeda," he whispered. "With Medusa's head in your hands."

Corbin stared at the vast mute wonder of the stars. He glanced anew overhead and traced the horizontal line of the Milky Way, where it swept out of the east, bolting across Perseus's back, through Cassiopeia's wobbly chair, to careen past the Northern Cross and fade into a throbbing glow, way out in the silence of the universe.

Far off, along the northern shoreline, only a few dim lights shimmered in the darkness. No boat lights twinkled or moved on the water.

The wind in the rigging caught his attention again. He stared up at the *Rubi-Yacht's* mast, where it flickered in the light of the northern sky's starglow.

"Esse est percipi," Janet had muttered. "What a quaint thought!"

"What are you reading?" he asked her.

"George Berkeley. Some eighteenth-century empiricist. What an obscurantist! 'To be is to be perceived,' he says. Anything not perceived doesn't exist. Do you believe that, Corbin?"

"I don't know."

"Do I exist when you don't perceive me?"

"Of course you do. Don't you perceive yourself?"

"Yes. But what happens when nobody else is perceiving you? We really don't exist, do we, except locked in ourselves? Maybe the old empiricist wasn't so loony after all."

"Maybe not," Corbin said.

" 'But we're always being perceived,' he adds, 'by an infinite perceiver, who perceives us when all other perceivers are absent or asleep.' " She shook her head in disagreement. "I can't believe that, but it makes you wonder, this *esse est percipi,* doesn't it?"

"Yes," he said. "It does."

Corbin glanced back into the darkness of the galley, where Jil lay sleeping. He could not see her, but he knew she was there. That she existed. And that he existed too.

"Esse est percipi," he whispered. He glanced up again at the mast and at the constellations glowing softly in the night sky. "I perceive you," he whispered. "I perceive all of you. Every silent one of you. But do you perceive me? And does anyone out there perceive both of us?" He scanned the stars, as if half-anticipating an answer.

He wondered. "Yet I exist and perceive that one day I will cease to exist, like Janet, and will exist only so long as Craig and Jil continue to remember me, if I should be so lucky.

"Why are you whispering?" he asked himself. "And to whom?" he paused, as he addressed that silent perceiver within the mystery of the self. Perhaps Berkeley was partly right but had reversed the true order of his insight. "To perceive is to be. *Percipere est esse!*" Corbin liked that better. "And isn't it enough that I should perceive Jil and find my existence inseparable from hers?"

Corbin reached up and touched the damp cover over the boom. He stared at the stars one final time. "*Esse est percipi*," he repeated. Then he descended into the darkness of the galley, lay down beside Jil, and covered the two of them with the sheet. He put his arm around her waist and lay there, listening to the wind in the rigging and to the murmuring of the water as it sloshed between the two hulls. His mind continued to rove the stars, as he listened to the wind and to the sound of Jil's breathing. And only toward early morning did he finally fall asleep.

chapter **sixteen**

"**C**orbin, honey! Wake up!"

The pungent aroma of coffee stung the edges of Corbin's consciousness. The brew's redolence permeated the galley and stirred Corbin's stomach to want its warmth and flavor.

"Corbin, are you awake?"

Corbin could sense the uneasiness in Jil's voice as well as in the nudging motion of her hand. Her fingers felt cold and stiff.

"It's beginning to drizzle," she said.

"What time is it?" he mumbled.

"Just a little past seven. Come on, get up."

Corbin rolled slowly in her direction and opened his eyes. Jil was standing on the cabin floor's sole. She had slipped into a yellow rubber raincoat. Its high turned-up collar swallowed her neck and ears; her reddish-blonde hair poked out around the corners of the collar.

The coat hung unzipped all the way down to her

thighs Corbin could see Jil's white blouse and white shorts beneath it. Her dark tan legs made his insides roll with contentment and desire. She smiled as he looked up past her legs and focused his eyes on her mouth and face.

"I've got coffee for you. And some warm water in a pan, for cereal."

"Good!" he mumbled. He groped for her and slipped his hands inside her opened coat. He put his arms about her waist and laid his face against her stomach. "Um, but you're warm!" he said.

"Corbin! The weather's getting serious. Listen!" She clicked on the radio.

". . . depression has been upgraded to a full tropical storm. It is expected to move through the Carolinas later this morning. Winds gusting to sixty-five miles per hour. Rain heavy at times. A cold front over the Ohio Valley should clear the storm by early evening.

"Current temperature in the low country is seventy-eight; sixty-eight in the mountains. Today's high should peak in the upper eighties.

"High tides along the coast will bring flooding to low-lying areas. Flash floods are likely in the upstate and mountains. Persons living near stream banks and creek bottoms are urged to observe extreme caution and remain alert. Violent winds are expected to bring down power lines across the state.

"A storm advisory has been issued for all counties in the low country. Sea winds steady at forty to fifty knots. Lake conditions across the state will deteriorate to poor to dangerous. Wind gusts over Lake Moultrie and Lake Murray may hit fifty knots; sixty as the storm progresses.

"The counterclockwise disturbance of the air has made winds unstable. A tornado watch is in effect along the storm's perimeter: from Augusta to Greenville to Charlotte and Florence.

"Small craft are advised to moor down or proceed with caution to nearest marinas.

"The disturbance along the South Atlantic coast has been upgraded to a storm. It is expected to move . . ."

Corbin reached up and flipped off the switch.

Jil ran her fingers slowly through Corbin's tangled hair.

"Please, Corby! I need to get back. Remember, I need to go to Florence, if possible."

"I understand," he said, as he stood beside her and kissed her worried face. "I'll have you under sail in no time."

Just then the boat yawed and the pan of hot water slid along the gas burner and spilled partially onto the companionway. Corbin pulled Jil back quickly to keep her from getting a burn. The coffee pot slid off its eye but wedged between the stove and the cabin's starboard wall.

"I'd better take a cup of that before it spills," Corbin said. "Then let's discuss what to do."

Corbin pulled on his shorts and shirt, slipped into his dock shoes, and climbed up into the cockpit.

A strong breeze blew steadily out of the southeast. A fine drizzle accompanied it and coated everything with its cool wetness. Dark furrowed clouds filled the sky in all directions. They moved rapidly across the lake, across the Spence Islands to the east, and on across the misty horizon to the north.

The water quivered in choppy wakes, but its waves were still small and free of white caps. Many dark patches of water indicated a changing and oscillating wind.

"Probably not blowing over ten to twelve knots," he said. "The big squalls haven't gotten here yet. I'd say we've got another two hours or more before the storm really sets in. Then neither of us will want to be out here."

Jil handed Corbin a Styrofoam cup half-filled with hot coffee. The coffee was extremely black and still emitted a thin vapor of steam.

"You can't tow me, can you?" Jil asked.

"There's no need for that. Besides, you're a good

sailor."

"I'd like to think so," she said, "but being with you makes me feel ... vulnerable." She put her face up to his damp cheek and kissed him, while he sipped his coffee.

"I'd say the fastest way to get home is to cross the lake here." He pointed to the south, "and hug the shoreline back through the channel," he turned and pointed to the southeast, "and then keep as close to the shore as you can until you get back to the dam. The trees will knock off most of the wind. From the dam, you can jibe back into the cove. Or just run with the wind."

"What if I just motor back and don't bother with the sails?"

"I think the ride will be smoother if you're sailing, at least with a jib. Remember, the motor has to *push* you; the wind will *lift* you. If the wind increases badly, the jib will be safer than having to fight the mainsail too. I've often come in on just a jib, especially if the wind is up."

"Sounds reasonable," she smiled. "When we first started sailing, Aiken often made me bring the boat back by myself, just in case someday I had to do it alone. He'd sit here in the cockpit," she nodded toward the starboard seat, "and explain the moves and would man the sheets and winches for me. Then, on mild days, he'd encourage me to take it out by myself, until I really had mastered it. But I hate sailing alone," she said, looking up at Corbin, "and don't really want to do it again, once we get back." She put her arms about his neck and kissed him hard on his stubbled chin. "You're getting wet," she said. "Let me get you a coat."

Corbin watched Jil return to the galley while he stood near the stern and began to survey the lake. He knew he should go back with her and not make her sail in alone. But he so wanted a few more hours to himself and one last run at the lake, however selfish that might seem.

A lone sea gull winged its way low across the water; it had come from the direction of the Spence Islands. It flew to the south of the *Columbia* and on around the sandy finger of Lunch Island's southeastern point. The bird settled in the choppy water about eighty yards off shore.

The coffee was strong and hot and tasted oily. Corbin preferred it with a touch of cream, but this would do, under the circumstances.

He noticed that the clouds were beginning to swirl and that misty eddies were forming along the clouds' trailing edges. He turned toward the northeast. A patch of sunlight suddenly burst through one such tatter over distant Goat Island. The sun's bright rays illumined the island's pines and flashed yellow upon the water. "Just maybe the forecasters were wrong," Corbin thought.

He could hear Jil sorting through the raingear in the forecastle.

"Extra large is all I have," she called.

"That'll do," he replied, as he gulped the coffee and began to feel the dampness and wetness of the drizzle, as it beaded up on his arms and hair. He ran his left hand through his hair. It was sopping wet.

"Here!" Jil said, as she struggled out of the galley and handed him one of Aiken's frayed rubber coats.

Corbin quickly pulled it on and hiked up its hood.

"I've got some oatmeal," she said, "and powdered milk. Care for any?"

"I'd love some," he smiled. "Then, we need to get you home."

"I'm not afraid," she said. "Come on and let's eat."

"OK."

Corbin followed her down the step, pushed back the hood, and sat against the aft bulkhead's cushion. He watched her prepare two bowls of instant oatmeal; he leaned out and poured himself a second cup of coffee.

"Jil, nothing can be the same again," he suddenly said. "I'll want you more than ever now. I'll want to wake up every morning with you. No matter where you are."

She sat the oatmeal on the table and handed him a plastic spoon. "Eat your breakfast," she said.

"Why are women so damn practical? I'm all but proposing to you."

"I know that," she said, as she sat down and looked across the settee at him. "But, I'm not going anywhere. We just need time, Corbin. That's all."

Corbin sank a spoon in the warm cereal and began to eat it hungrily. He wanted to make a comment about the cereal, about her hair, about how much he wanted to see her in the kitchen and hallway and bedrooms of the pagoda house in Long Creek. But he knew he had to keep silent and wait, however long that might take. So he sat there and finished the cereal, then leaned over the table and kissed her.

After breakfast, Corbin set about to cast off Jil's boat.

"Jil, I've flipped on your running lights," he said, as he nodded in the direction of the light panel. "Don't forget to press them off, or the battery will run down."

"I'll remember. I hope!" she smiled.

"Sure!"

He climbed back out to the cockpit and raised the lid on the sail locker. A thin stream of water dripped into the compartment. He leaned down and pulled out the jib bag and closed the lid as quickly as possible.

Corbin stepped up on the port bench and pulled himself on deck. He squeezed inside the shroud lines and laid the bag down on the foredeck. He began to bend on the jib. Its sheets came unwound, but he bunched them back up until he had laid out the sail. Then he snapped its tack to the bow fixture and began clipping the snap shackles onto the stay. He fastened the head to the jib halyard and began laying out the sheets. He threaded the starboard sheet through its fairlead block and laid it back along the decktrack and did the same for the port sheet. All Jil would have to do was raise the jib, once she was safely free of the island.

He rolled up her jib bag and carried it back to the locker. He dropped it in to the right of her gas tank, then closed the lid. Finally, Corbin leaned out over the stern, lowered her outboard, and raised the lid a second time. He primed the pump, dropped the lid, and started the motor. He set it on idle and listened to it whine and sputter.

"Whenever you're ready, I'll lift your anchor and undo this cord," he said, nodding toward the line that he had used to tie the two boats together.

Jil came up out of the galley and looked at him,

then looked away. How he wished he could take her in and somehow come back for his own boat, with time left to sail, but that would be impossible.

"I hate to leave you like this," he said. "I know I'm being selfish. I shouldn't have made you stay over night."

"Nobody made me do anything," she said, "that I didn't want to do."

He came toward her and kissed her. "Here," he said, as he slipped off Aiken's coat. "I'm going to raise your anchor now and cast off."

Corbin hurried forward to the bow pulpit and drew up the anchor. He secured in to the anchor stock on the pulpit and returned to the cockpit. Hopping across to the *Rubi-Yacht*'s stern, he began loosening the cord.

Jil had taken a seat beside the transom; her hand lay extended over the stern; she put the motor on reverse, and the *Columbia* slowly began to back away.

Corbin walked along toward his own hatch, hopped up on the port seat, and pushed with his foot at the *Columbia*'s rubrail as the boat crept past and eased away from the *Rubi-Yacht*'s hull. The boat swung free and, with its stern facing Corbin, began to motor away from his craft and from the shallows of the island. Jil looked back and waved to him; he waved to her, as her boat slipped slowly into the misty drizzle and toward the distant southern shore. He could see her white stern light as the boat bobbed and dipped in the water. Then the light grew pale and faint and appeared to blink as the boat pulled ever farther away. Corbin could see Jil climb toward the cabin to hoist the jib. But he was beginning to get wet and feel cold, so he waved one last time, then hurried below for his own rain gear.

chapter **seventeen**

     Corbin paused in the galley to check the contents of the Styrofoam chest. He had set the container on the dinette table after returning the sloshing chest to the *Rubi-Yacht* following the meal in Jil's boat. He had leaned the bag of corn chips against it, but the bag had slid off onto a seat.

  Corbin pried off the chest's lid and peered inside. The bottle of Chardonnay had fallen over and its label had come unglued. It came off in his fingers when he nudged the bottle. The sandwiches remained where he had stacked them to keep dry atop the beer cans. The sandwiches looked fresh, though moisture had formed inside the plastic wrappers. The carton of potato salad floated in the water; the package of beef sticks had settled to the bottom. Only the jar of pickles appeared unaffected.

  The water felt cool as he slipped his hand in and wrestled out a Coke. A little extra caffeine wouldn't hurt, he thought. He pressed the lid down tight and set the chest in the sink.

Just then he felt a cold oozing sensation in his shoes. He glanced down at his feet, where the carpet covering the cabin's floor appeared wet. He could feel the rug squishing under his feet. Corbin bent down to discover that the carpet was soaking wet. He could pat the water with his hand.

He stepped into the forecastle to inspect its floor. Everything there was dry, as it should be, except the carpet felt clammy and damp. He glanced overhead to see if he had left the cabin's "head" hatch raised. He had, but no moisture dripped from it.

Corbin turned toward the galley and its open hatchway. "You should have closed it," he rebuked himself. "Rain must have trickled in during the night." Or had it? "Could I have damaged the centerboard or the keel?" he wondered. "Or cracked the hull?" Neither of the latter seemed likely. Or even possible.

He would have to take up the carpet and mop it out when he returned to the marina. Right now he wanted to put on his rain gear and sail, at least for an hour or so, before the storm struck. Sailing in anything like Nova Scotia's "seas" was rare on the lake, except during blustery days or on the occasion of a passing storm. In two hours, or less, he would easily be home, safe in the sailing club's Back Cove.

Now, he wanted to sail, to tack about the lake and run with the wind.

He popped open the Coke, took a drink, and set the can on the W.C lid. He would soon need to use that himself, he thought. He took down his foul-weather gear from its peg in the hanging locker, sat back on the V-bunk, and pulled the rubberized pants over his shorts.

Before fastening them, he used the W.C., then slipped into the large yellow jacket and squeezed back out into the galley. He took a few fast draughts of the Coke and dropped the can into the plastic bag beneath the sink.

The drizzle had let up by the time he reemerged in the cockpit. He knew the rain would commence anew, but he decided to leave his coat's hood down until it did. He could feel sweat gathering already on his arms and under his shirt.

He sat on the starboard seat and glanced across the choppy water toward Jil's diminishing vessel. In ten minutes or less, she would pass through the channel, and, if she caught the wind just right, should have a decent tack back to the dam and be in the marina within an hour.

Jil was quite unlike Janet; yet he found her as loving and as desirous as Janet had ever been. Jil was taller, physically stronger, and sensually assertive, while

Janet had been reserved and cautious. Yet the two shared a common characteristic. Jil displayed an independence equal to anything Janet had possessed.

How he hoped Jil would marry him! If and when Aiken should *die!* Damn! But he felt miserable to wish his own friend's death! My God, Corbin! he sighed to himself. What am I to do? He took a deep breath.

"Whatever happens, I will not lose you," he mumbled. "I will not lose you, Jil Hunter. I love you too much," he sighed.

He rose and began to unsnap the blue slip that covered the mainsail and boom. He untied the back end and climbed on deck and unfastened the snaps and string about the mast. The cover slid off onto the hatch and fell into the galley.

The cabin's hatch was very wet, and Corbin almost fell overboard when he tripped on its grabrail as he bent forward to hop down into the cockpit. He caught hold of the handrail just in time, as his body slapped hard against the port side of the hull. He slowly pulled himself back up onto the toerail and climbed back into the cockpit. You'd better watch out! he thought. And be more careful next time. He rubbed his arm and side as the pain slowly went away.

Corbin gathered up the slipcover and stuffed it in the sail locker. He pulled out his jib bag and proceeded forward again. This time he was more cautious and circumspect. Laying the bag on the hatch, he rolled it toward the mast, and then mounted the cabin roof.

He went about his work and soon had the jib snapped in place and fastened to its halyard. He wanted to go on and weigh anchor, but the wind appeared to be up, "and the boat will surely drift," he told himself. "Better wait." Even if it meant having to track back up again.

He held to the mast as he slipped between it and the shrouds, noting that the telltale ribbons were already beginning to stand out. He glanced in the direction of the wind. It was bearing out of the south-to-southwest and had picked up considerably. He judged it to be blowing about fifteen knots. Small whitecaps were beginning to form across the lake and all across the water between the *Rubi-Yacht* and the Spence Islands. The waves were still low, however, and big patches of dark, wrinkled water rippled between them at noticeable intervals.

"The sailing will be perfect," he thought. "If only it will hold like this for an hour!"

The boat was beginning to pitch when Corbin finally cranked up the outboard. He listened to the motor hum until he was satisfied that it would not suddenly die on him, then he set the throttle on idle, lowered the centerboard about twelve turns, carefully made his way up to the bow, and began to haul in the anchor. As soon as he had mounted it in its slot on the pulpit, he fed the rope down into the forehatch, then turned and hoisted the jib. He fastened its halyard quickly in place and made his way back to the stern. He raised the sail locker lid, pulled out the spare halyard piece he had used to tie his and Jil's boat together, and fastened it to the end of the tiller's fold-out extension. He closed the lid, sat down, and pulled the tiller in, so the boat would swing to starboard. Sliding the gearshift lever to forward, he arced the boat around in a slow, two-hundred-degree turn.

Corbin motored away from, but at an oblique angle to, the island. The wind now struck him head-on and made the ribbons fly straight out. He cut the motor off, locked it in place, then hurried forward to raise the mainsail. He belayed the halyard to its cleat and returned to the helm. The wind struck the sails across the port bow and billowed the jib out with a clean snap. Corbin quickly trimmed and looped its sheet about the starboard winch and sailed the boat in a southwest-to-west direction.

He rounded the island's long sandy finger, and guided the boat parallel to the island, but at a good hundred-yard's distance from the shore. A following wind now blew over the port quarter, and as Corbin let out the sheets, the wind bore the *Rubi-Yacht* smartly along. The island, with its intermittent clay embankments and sandy beaches, its pines and mantle of sedges and sumac, slipped slowly and gracefully away from the starboard bow.

Corbin soon passed the island and ran cleanly with the wind. He fed out both the main and jib sheets stingily and aimed the boat in a general west-to-northwest direction. His compass registered a 300-degree bearing.

The boat slipped smoothly through the water and slowly cut past each rolling wave. He estimated that the winds were building between twenty to twenty-two knots and that the *Rubi-Yacht* was moving close to hull speed. Soon enough he would need to reverse his course and tack back to the east. But he wanted to delay that maneuver until he had to, for, once in, he doubted if he would get back for at least another two weeks. He simply had too many commitments he could no longer postpone and appointments he could not cancel.

He listened to the water splash vigorously along the hull and to the wind whipping the halyards in a steady beat against the mast. It created an eerie but melodious noise, one he had come to love and await with anticipation each sail. Now he wanted it to last as long as possible. And the fact that the clouds were heavy and low and about to rain had no bearing at all on his instinct. He would take the rain in stride, too, when it came.

He thought again of his workload at the office and wondered how their youngest partner, Andrew Telford, was doing.

"Andy, how's it going?" he had asked the junior associate. He and Slaygard had hired him earlier the past month. Corbin had high hopes for him. They had assigned him all their new drug cases, and he had successfully defended two out of three, to date.

"Oh, just fine, sir," the young man had replied. Andrew was a tall, slender, black-haired, twenty-five-year old. His newly framed license to practice law hung proudly between his college and law school diplomas. The eyes of his young wife surveyed his desk from her tilted lavender frame beside his telephone.

"She's very lovely," Corbin said.

"Yeah! We've only been married six weeks," he grinned.

"Enjoy it," Corbin smiled.

The Moving Finger writes, and, having writ,
Moves on . . .

He looked at Andy and back at the photograph a second time. "Tell me about the case coming up. Is it winnable?"

"Yes, sir. I just interviewed the fellow again yesterday. He's been charged with possession with intent to distribute crack."

"You're becoming a regular pro at this," Corbin interjected.

"Not really. But I think we've got a good chance to win. I tried to get his charges dismissed at the preliminary, but it didn't work. We select the jury tomorrow."

"That'll be the key."

"I know. I've learned that middle-aged moms, school teachers, state office workers, and small business owners come down the hardest on druggers."

"What's the best defense you've got going for him?"

"Well, I've thought about it an awful lot. First off, he's a grad student at the university. Ph.D. candidate in physics. Now, most of those guys are clean. That's a fact. I did some research. They're not about to play around with their crania. That's fact one.

"Fact two. He was pulled for speeding in a hospital zone. He was running late for a lab he was supposed to be supervising, but he was running late because he had gotten stuck behind an ambulance heading for this very hospital.

"Fact three. *His* car was in the shop. Mind you, *his* car. He had borrowed a coed's car, whose roommate he was dating. Ah!" he grinned. "That ought to be worth something!"

Corbin smiled.

"Fact four. When they pulled the stuff from the trunk, he didn't even know what it was. He's even willing to undergo a polygraph, if necessary.

"So. Not his car! Not his cocaine! Not his girl! And, most of all, not his style! I've even checked his family's medical record back through the sixth grade. Clean! Perfectly clean!"

"Who's hearing the case?"

"Judge Plesser."

"He's wily. He's a tough act to handle."

"I know. But he's heard the other cases I've defended. I think he's beginning to respect me. Maybe."

"Have you talked to prosecution?"

"Yes. They've nothing really unfavorable other than the speeding charges in a hospital zone. They're just under pressure. The whole system's under pressure to prosecute drugs."

"Good luck with it."

"Thank you."

Corbin glanced again at the young woman in the photograph. "Have you taken her out recently? I mean, really out? To somewhere super special? So she feels special?"

"No, sir. I've been pretty occupied, I guess."

"Well, I'm making reservations for you Friday night at the Elite Epicurean. Steak. Wine. The works. Whatever. Just promise me one thing."

"Yes?"

"When you clink your classes together, say, 'For God Boy!' "

" 'For God Boy!' " he smiled.

"Good luck again. I'll not see you till Monday."

"Thank you, sir."

"Andy, the honor is mine. And, please, stop calling me, 'Sir!' OK?"

"Yes, sir! I understand."

"Yes, I can see that you do."

chapter **eighteen**

C orbin estimated that he had easily run two miles in a northwestwardly direction beyond the windward tip of Lunch. Pine-crowned Wessinger Island had dropped aft to starboard, and the long, tree-lined shoal of Shull lay to port. The two promontories hugged the lake's dark horizon and hovered dimly in the mist.

The wind had increased; the *Rubi-Yacht* hummed along at near hull-speed. The sloop cut cleanly through the curling waves and sighed restlessly as it passed them. Corbin sat on the starboard bench and watched the swells recede sternward as the boat yawed along. Overhead, the clouds had blackened; once more drizzle fell.

Corbin eased the mainsheet in while steering the *Rubi-Yacht* into a beam reach. He took one wrap of the jib sheet off the starboard winch and pulled the tiller in, forcing the rudder to the left. As he did, Corbin let the starboard jibsheet run free. The boat swung boldly about to its left and headed into the wind at a close starboard reach. The jib luffed and the boat rocked as Corbin swiftly cranked the port jibsheet in. Then the main swung over and stiffened as the jib caught the wind and popped out in a smooth arc. Both jib and mainsail cupped to port. Corbin set the boat on a southeast bearing and began the long tack homeward, back across the darkening lake.

Running with the wind had been effortless; now the reverse was true. Oncoming waves slapped against the *Rubi-Yacht's* bow and, kicking up spray, rolled past the hull. The halyards rattled noisily, and the wind, jetting in from the jib's curled sail, moaned against the mast. The waves rose in broken syncopation, forming whitecaps along their collapsing crests.

Come away, hey! Corbin thought to himself.

It began to rain.

The first drops splattered against the yacht, sounding like pellets of hail striking tin. They clattered against the boom and off the hatch. Then a veil of rain swept the deck and caused the boat to rock.

Corbin loosened the main sheet to control the rocking, and scanned the lake for the next sheet of rain. He could hear it splattering on the water and see it descending in flickering droplets before it crossed the foredeck and danced off the bow. Corbin tightened the main sheet and trapped the wind and rain simultaneously against the sail; the boat heeled slightly, but caught a second lift before the gust blew on. As it passed, it drenched the cockpit with rain.

The waves began to mount in two-foot swells; each measured three to four feet from crest to bottom of trough. Each struck the bow head on with a rhythmic thud and spewed spray up over the cockpit and down the decktrack to Corbin's left. Rain running off the sail formed a gleaming stream as it cascaded off the boom.

Corbin tightened his hood about his face and watched the falling rain eddy down the drainspout at his feet. His shoes were soaked. Water dripped from his left hand and ran down the tiller arm toward the transom.

Suddenly, the wind changed direction and began to blow in from the south. The boat heeled sharply as the wind hit its sails full abeam. Corbin immediately loosened his port sheet and held the tiller steady. The boat corrected its course as the jib billowed clean again and Corbin tacked eastward. His bearing now lay between eighty-five to ninety degrees on the compass, with Shull and Lunch Islands to starboard and to his south.

"Five miles to port," he told himself. "I will bear toward Ballentine, tack southeast, pass between Goat and the Spence Islands, then make for home. You should be in the harbor within two hours," he whispered to himself.

Just then he glanced off in the direction of the Spence Islands. A pale, faint, angle of sail flickered momentarily on the horizon. "Could it be Jil?" he wondered. Had she been forced back by the storm. But it was raining so, he could not tell.

A wall of water struck the starboard bow and raked the deck and hatch with its spray. Corbin turned his face to the left, just as the spray hit his coat and ran freely off his hood, coat, and legs.

He glanced again toward the distant, heeling sail. He was too far off to recognize whose boat it was. He tightened the jib and main sheets slightly and sailed as close into the wind as possible without allowing the sails to luff.

An abrupt lull in the wind caused the sails to sag and the boat to pitch heavily into the next few waves. Suddenly a calm descended upon the waters, accompanied by a violent downpour of rain. Corbin inched his way along the tiller, extended its fold-out arm forward, and, leaning hard on the rope, let himself down into the galley.

Water streamed off the cockpit seats and gurgled loudly down the drainspout. He stepped all the way down into the galley to shield himself from the rain. A rush of cold water lapped against his shoes. He glanced at his feet. The cabin floor shimmered in an inch or more of dark water. "Where is it coming from? Where?" he wondered. It had to be coming in from around the keel or centerboard. But he did not know which.

The violent squall subsided and the rain with it. Once more the wind struck up again. The boat yawed and the centerboard began to hum. Corbin climbed back out to the cockpit, sat down and slid aft along the starboard bench, until he could grasp the tiller in hand.

The distant sail loomed larger now; Corbin could make out the boat's arched jib as well as its mainsail. The boat rose and fell in time with the waves. It was not Jil. Whoever's boat it was, its skipper was running wing and wing and heading directly toward the *Rubi-Yacht*.

As it drew closer, Corbin could make out its hull. It was white with green markings and green streamers on its upper shrouds. Its tall mast twinkled in the rain as its cables and halyards trembled against the background of the distant, dark horizon. Its red bow light blinked as the boat cut through the running swells.

It was Oren Medlow!

"What in the world can Medlow want?" Corbin wondered. He knew he was a much better sailor than

Medlow. Medlow had no business being out here. "You ass!" Corbin mumbled. "You are crazier than I thought."

Corbin eased his boat closer into the wind to accommodate Medlow's approach. He wondered if Medlow had brains to do the same. Corbin watched his wind indicator carefully, as well as the waves, for any further change in wind direction. All too rapidly Medlow's *Century* approached. Corbin had to luff to keep out of his way. His boom swayed loosely overhead.

"You ass!" he hollered as Medlow drew into sight.

"Ass, nothing!" Medlow bellowed in reply. "Jil said I'd find you here."

"What's happened?" Corbin called.

"Aiken! He's dead! Died last night. Cerebral hemorrhage. Jil wants you to meet her in the Back Cove."

The *Century* was now only yards away and hissed rapidly past Corbin's port side.

"Wait up!" Medlow bellowed again, as he began to jibe around Corbin's stern and come up along his windward side.

Corbin watched the smart green and white hull swing the corner and tack back along to starboard.

"You shouldn't be out here!" he yelled to Medlow.

"The hell you say!" Medlow roared. "I'm as good

a sailor as you are, any day! You don't own this damn lake. It belongs to us all!"

Corbin stared at the ruddy man's face. Medlow was clad to the neck in rain gear, much like himself. "You're a fool!" he wanted to say, but said nothing.

"Two hundred says I can beat you to port!" Medlow grinned. "If you're so damn good, prove it!"

"You're crazy! Some other time! My bilge is leaking!"

"What's wrong, lover boy? Lost your mettle?"

"Up yours!" retorted Corbin. He realized there was no point in explaining. "I can beat you with one hand tied behind my back," he boasted in anger.

"Then do it!" hollered Medlow, as his boat's mast pulled abeam of Corbin's and passed Corbin's, causing his sails to be cut off from the incoming wind. "Up whose, now?" he laughed, as he pointed toward Ballentine Cove. "First to the marker, then to the spillway, then home!"

Medlow's boat slipped past and left Corbin in the *Century's* dirty air.

"Damn!" Corbin moaned. He had wanted only to return to the marina and be with Jil. Poor Aiken, he thought. However much he wanted Jil, he still felt sorry for Aiken. And tremendously guilty.

Corbin sat forward and watched Medlow's boat slowly pull away. It would be all he could do to catch up with him now, especially since he had taken the windward advantage.

"Enjoy it, while you can!" Corbin whispered. "I will retake you, if it's the last thing I do!"

The *Rubi-Yacht* pitched and yawed in the *Century's* wake and dropped behind its stern.

Patience! Corbin thought to himself. Just watch the wind and be patient.

Corbin knew he had to seize upon a plan. He had to formulate a means by which, first, he could overtake Medlow and, second, determine where on the lake such a maneuver would most likely succeed. But it had to be soon. However little his heart might be in it.

The waves struck both boats hard from starboard. Whitecaps lapped everywhere in the darkness of the storm. Corbin could even discern Medlow's stern light, as it blinked between oncoming waves.

The howling wind oscillated between a close reach and a beam reach. Corbin could hear it groaning against the mast. Corbin watched Medlow's boat heel heavily in the gusts and observed the bright wrinkle that fluttered and formed vertically along the *Century's* tall mainsail.

"His sails are entirely too full!" Corbin realized. "Entirely too full!"

Rain coursed down the big sail and spun wildly

off the boom. With that much drag on Medlow's sail, Corbin knew he could overtake him. If granted enough time. "But in this storm, where, when, and how?"

Corbin glanced ahead. The *Century* bore slightly to starboard of distant Goat Island. The boat's green and white hull was closing in on precisely that mark where Corbin knew the first buoy rode anchored in shallow water. Medlow would reach the marker first. "But let him!" he thought. "He will be coming in too fast! Coming in too sharply. And if he doesn't run aground, he will have to veer to his left. And when he does, he'll make too great a swing around the marker. And that's when I can take him!"

All Corbin had to do was to hang back. To stay just beyond range of the *Century's* turbulence. And tack to windward the instant Medlow's stern cleared the marker.

Spray hissed across Corbin's bow and danced crazily through the shrouds. Once again the wind rattled the halyards and moaned in the cupped recesses of the sails. Waves thudded against the *Rubi-Yacht's* hull and caused the vessel to yaw and heel. Corbin loosened the main sheet and brought the sloop slowly out of the heel. Spray slammed against the hatch and drenched Corbin from head to foot.

Corbin played the tiller out to starboard. He

trimmed the mainsail in, by a small increment, and pulled leeward and then astern of Medlow's craft. He waved impishly as he gained ever so slightly.

"Make him think you're going to pass him! Make him sail high to the end!" Corbin told himself.

Medlow glanced in his direction and began to tighten his mainsail. He pulled on his jib sheet and pushed his own tiller away. The action increased the *Century's* speed to its maximum hull velocity.

"Look at him go!" smiled Corbin, as rain spattered noisily on the water and the wind drove it across the decks in stinging sheets. Water swirled off the boom and momentarily blinded Corbin.

Just then the white shoal marker bobbed into view. At first, less than eighty yards away. Then sixty! Forty! Medlow immediately veered to his port to avoid too fast an approach, but, in the instant he did, Corbin headed to windward and sailed closehaulded for Medlow's stern.

The *Century* slowed and began its yawing tack. But it was too late. The boat rocked and swept past the marker in a wide graceful arc. The *Rubi-Yacht* caught the lift, cleared the buoy on the marker's portside, and pulled abeam of the *Century*. Medlow's boat slowed even more as it heeled spectacularly in the turn.

Corbin felt a little guilty, for he had shaved "the

room at the mark rule" a little closely. But damn! He was entitled to any room freely given. In any event, the lead was his. And he had earned it.

The *Rubi-Yacht* was to windward. Once through the channel, it was straight across the lake. Turn at the spillway. And run for home. All he had to do was to keep in front. Watch the wind. And stay between Medlow and the next marker.

As Corbin sailed into the channel, he glanced to port to monitor Medlow's pursuit. The big green and white hull had yet to climb out of its heel. Its large white sails bulged with wind. Medlow had only to flatten the sails and ease off on the main, but he seemed oblivious to the maneuver or unable to execute it effectively on his own. Corbin did not know which.

The wind oscillated from the south to the southeast. Corbin thought at first that he was caught in the leeward turbulence of the Spence Islands, but the flattened swells undulating in the lake indicated otherwise. The wrinkled dark patches that raced across the water signaled an unmistakable shift in the wind. Corbin picked it up and steered to port and caught a strong lift from the gust.

The lift propelled the *Rubi-Yacht* with an audible sigh and hiss from the spray. Corbin handled the helm as deftly as he knew how and steered the boat, closehauled, directly toward the distant spillway's storm-darkened shore.

Slowly the *Rubi-Yacht* pulled ahead. The *Century's* sails sagged momentarily as Corbin's boat cut off the wind. Medlow's big boat began to pitch and yaw and slam, bow hard, into the mounting waves.

"A half-length! A whole! Two!" Corbin counted them, as the *Rubi-Yacht* pulled away.

Corbin glanced back at Medlow himself.

The realtor's grimacing face was framed resolutely in a mound of hunkered-down yellow rain gear that glistened wet with spray and the sparkle of rain. You will not catch me, now! Corbin thought. No matter how hard you try! Not now!

Corbin kept his eye on the lake and watched for the slightest shift in wind.

The rain had been falling steadily for some time. It descended in angled, measured sheets, as gust after gust swept across the lake. Formidable waves slammed relentlessly against Corbin's bow, kicking spray high up into the jib and spilling it, wind-raked, across the decks. The wind shrieked in the sails as thirty-knot gales slapped at the cloths. The entire craft trembled, while the mast groaned and vibrated to the roar of the howling winds.

He turned once more to check on Medlow. Medlow seemed absorbed in clinging to his tiller and leaning out to starboard as the *Century's* hull kept yawing and careening to port at an incredible speed. Corbin could not help but feel sorry for him. "You'll learn!" he thought to himself. "The hard way!"

"Tack on a header!" God boy had always said. "Tack high! Tack on a wave! Tack quickly! Stay out of troughs! And you'll never go down in a race or storm."

Easier said than done, Corbin mused. And more easily executed with a crew than alone.

Corbin studied the surface of the waves for new wind shifts. Whitecaps undulated in blinking syncopation all across the east, south, and southeast. A ruffled patch of water materialized off the starboard bow. The wave in front of it had formed a long, white rolling crest. "What a header!" he uttered, as he tacked into it. He trimmed the mainsail and began counting. "Twelve. Eighteen. Twenty!" He tacked again at the next oscillation of wind, confident he would easily stay now between Medlow and the mark.

"It is just a matter of time!" he told himself. He cocked his head to port to locate his adversary. Medlow appeared as a yellow blob bobbing along in the back of the hull of the leaning green and white vessel. The sky behind him was absolutely black. The sails were etched in gray.

He glanced at his watch. "Eleven-thirty!" he muttered. He and Medlow had been at this for an hour and a half. He was grateful it would soon be over.

Corbin realized how tired his left arm felt and, rubbing it with his right hand, began manning the helm with both hands. "Thirsty!" An insatiable thirst irritated the walls of his gullet. He longed for a cup of water or a gulp of Coke. Either would do.

"Why not?" he thought, as he began to slide forward and grope for the wet cord. He folded out the tiller's extension arm, leaned into the tied halyard, and staggered windward toward the galley. He stepped down on the centerboard's crank box and, holding to the tiller's cord, swayed out in the direction of the chest. Just then water sloshed on the cabin floor, and he glanced down.

A panicky sickness swept over him! "Four! Five! How many inches?" he groaned, as he stared at the swirling water on the floor. "You must get to port! As quickly as possible!" he said to himself.

He reached for the Styrofoam chest and popped off its lid. The latter splashed in the water and began to float in the passageway. Corbin yanked out a Coke and hauled himself back up and out of the galley and returned to his starboard post.

"What should I do?" he wondered, as he fumbled

for the wet tiller with his cold left hand.

He would soon be approaching the spillway marker.

"Too late to cut off now," he told himself. "You're in it to the end."

He wedged the can between his leggings and peeled off its key. He put the can to his lips and downed the Coke in two long gurgling draughts. He wiped his mouth and threw the can into the galley.

He clenched his lips, looked for the marker, and began to jibe. The *Rubi-Yacht* heeled to starboard, cut past the buoy, and rolled out heavily around the marker. Corbin could hear the water sloshing in the cabin as he made the turn.

The wind whistled across the stern and forced him to sail wing on wing, his boom to the right and jib to the left. Both sails ballooned out full, wet, and heavy with rain. Suddenly a loud twang hummed beneath the hull and rattled back underneath the cockpit. The rattling shook the boat violently and began working its way toward the transom. Waves splashed into the back of the boat, as the *Rubi-Yacht* slowed and scudded sluggishly through the water. The mast vibrated and the jib began to luff. Suddenly, the noise ceased and a long white board popped up in the swirling eddies behind the rudder. It was his centerboard!

Corbin floundered in the cockpit for want of knowing what to do.

The boat drifted parallel to the dam's five huge concrete floodgates. Corbin watched them slip past, one by one, about forty yards off starboard bow. He grasped the tiller, trimmed hard on the mainsail, and steered the vessel slowly away from the angry rocks that jutted all along the dam's wall.

The boat's mast whined in the wind as the sails fluttered and flopped and the *Rubi-Yacht* limped sideways toward the Back Cove.

Just then Medlow's boat swung about the marker and came boldly into view. Medlow was sitting hunched up to starboard near the transom, holding to the traveler, and looking beaten and wan. He raised his hand in a formal salute as he passed Corbin but seemed indifferent to the *Rubi-Yacht's* stricken condition. He seemed to stare bewildered at Corbin; his face loomed drained of anger or defiance. A thin smirk creased his lips, but that was all.

"What an oblivious ass!" thought Corbin. "You poor wretch!"

Corbin watched him sail on toward the cove and maneuvered his own vessel toward calmer waters as fast as the boat would go. He unwrapped the port jib sheet, tossed it forward, and, hurrying toward the hatch, clambered on deck. He unfastened the jib halyard and let the jib sink flutteringly across the pulpit and bow, then began lowering the mainsail. He literally clawed it down into the galley until the wind could rake the sails no more.

"Ahhh!" he rolled to his side with a sigh. "What a note to end on!"

He sat up and tried to clear his mind for what next to do. Should he motor on into the marina, or dive beneath the hull and inspect the keel? He put his hands to his eyes and rubbed his tired face.

Suddenly, he thought of Jil! Of Aiken! Of course! He had to motor on in. That was exactly what he should do.

He scooted off the hatch and made his way wearily toward the stern.

chapter **nineteen**

A light steady rain had settled in upon the lake's cove. It fell with pointillistic precision upon the slate-gray waves and pattered softly across the *Rubi-Yacht's* hatch. Gusts of wind flapped the edges of the jib and kicked up wisps of spray. The cove's choppy waters slapped against the *Rubi-Yacht's* hull and abated with an echo.

Corbin paused by the galley to assess the water's depth where it sloshed in the cabin's sole. The dank mildewed odor of the cabin wafted on the galley's air and mingled with the musty scent of rain. Corbin inhaled it and stared inside. The dark water in the cabin washed against the dinette and ebbed across the cushions.

Just then the loud clapping of Medlow's sails distracted Corbin's inspection. Corbin craned his neck toward Medlow's boat. The *Rubi-Yacht* was drifting windward, about forty feet off the *Century's* starboard bow.

Medlow had secured his mainsail, or, at least, had

succeeded in collapsing it on top of his hatch; the stocky man was staggering into the wind, his head bowed toward his mast. Violent gusts snapped the jib noisily. Medlow grabbed hold of the mast and began unfastening the jib halyard. Only something seemed wrong. There was something strained, inappropriate, about his movements.

Medlow appeared to be caught on the inner shroud line; his yellow hood had slipped off his head. His thin black hair hung in matted strands over his sweaty balding head. His face was twisted in a grimace. It intermittently winced with pain and droll expressions of stupor. Suddenly, Medlow lurched sideways, groped for the mast, and crumpled on the foredeck amidst the clatter of the descending jib.

"A heart attack!" Corbin muttered.

Corbin stripped off his clammy weather gear; he mounted the port seat, kicked off his shoes, straddled the lifeline, and, teetering momentarily on the gunnel, dove into the water. He surfaced in a lapping wave that washed over him, but a second hurled him suddenly against the *Century*. He braced himself against its hull and swam into a third wave that swept him up against the transom. He grasped its ladder in both hands and pulled himself slowly up its rungs.

As Corbin climbed over into the stern, the winds picked up again and rocked the *Century* to and fro.

Corbin paused to catch his breath, then fingertipped his way along the starboard seat, and struggled atop the hatch. He clasped the wet handrail in both hands and crawled across the cabin to the mast.

The boat lurched again. As it did, Medlow's torso slid starboard and struck the rail of the pulpit; his legs slipped precariously out over the bow.

"Hold on, Medlow!" Corbin called. "I'm almost to you."

Medlow rolled to his left and held up an arm to Corbin. His mouth trembled as he spoke. "Corbin! Is it you?"

"Yes!" said Corbin, as he stretched his arm forward and clasped the sick man's hand in his own. "Hold tight! You're going to make it! It's all right!"

Medlow's brow had paled; his cheeks were sallow; the whites of his eyes appeared a milky blue. The stricken man raised a limp arm and laid it weakly on Corbin's shoulder and hugged him with what strength he possessed. "Forgive me!" he uttered. There were tears in his eyes.

"You're going to be all right!" Corbin whispered. "Damn, but I have hated you!" he smiled, as he dragged Medlow toward the mast.

"I'm going to tie you here!" Corbin said. "With this sheet!" he held up the starboard jib sheet. "Just lie still, until I can get you into the Back Cove."

Medlow's lips mumbled a silent "thank you" as Corbin wrapped the sheet carefully about his legs and body and tied it about the mast.

"Just don't move," Corbin said.

He patted the man on his shoulder, returned backward down across the hatch, and moved quickly toward the stern. He lowered Medlow's outboard into the water, primed his motor, and started it after several pulls. Corbin revved it up amidst the oily blue fumes of its popping exhaust and guided the *Century* toward the channel markers that led to the harbor.

As he motored in the marina's direction, he glanced back over his shoulder toward his own boat. The wind's intensity had dropped over the cove, and the rain had turned into a misty drizzle. Angry waves still lapped out in the lake but had subsided where they collided with the cove's choppy water.

A feeling of anguish came over him. There it was! Listing to port! Its gunwales at the waterline. And the wind blowing it slowly and heavily toward the causeway's rocks.

"Surely you can make it back!" he told himself. "You must make it back!" he said aloud, as he revved up the throttle and purled the hull's bow through the cove's black, puckered, silky water.

Corbin steered the *Century* past each marker and guided the classy fiberglass boat slowly toward the marina. The boat's big hull splashed quietly past the lily pads and sent them undulating up and down as the vessel's wake rippled through them.

As the entrance to the marina came into view, Corbin could see Jil standing on the end of the dock, searching the cove for his return. She looked confused. He knew she had not expected to see Medlow's boat first.

He waved to her and stood up slowly in the cockpit, so she would immediately recognize him. He waved a second time and pointed to Medlow's bundled form on the foredeck. He watched her return his wave, though her face still bore the marks of uncertainty.

The sailboat motored hoarsely into the calmer waters of the marina. The outboard's drone echoed forlornly off the moored vessels, as the *Century's* green and white hull passed each.

Corbin listened to the big boat's wake sigh as it rippled against the docked craft and rocked them faintly, one by one. A second person had now joined Jil. It was Harmond.

"Harmond! Jil!" Corbin called. "Oren's had a heart attack! He's still conscious. I need help."

The two of them hurried along the dockway as the *Century* passed.

"I haven't put the fenders down," Corbin said. "Get ready to help me dock!"

Harmond motioned for him to cut the motor. Corbin did and began to press the tiller slowly to his right. The *Century* slowed and began drifting in a wide quiet arc to Oren's slip. Harmond hurried out on the dock and waited for the boat to angle in, then as it scooted against the pads and bumped into the berth, he secured one of its dock lines about its cleat.

"I'll call the rescue squad," Harmond said. "Jil, quick! Get a blanket on Medlow. There's probably one in his forecastle. Hurry, before he goes into shock!"

"Corbin, are you all right?" Jil asked. "Where's the *Rubi-Yacht*? What happened?"

"I'll tell you later! Is the *Columbia's* hatch unlocked?"

"Yes! Why?"

"Is your dinghy aboard?"

"Yes, I'm pretty sure. But it's in the sail locker."

"I want you and Harmond to take over. I've got to get back to the *Rubi-Yacht*. It's still unanchored in the cove."

Corbin leaned out and helped Jil aboard. He kissed her and pressed her hands in his.

"I'm sorry about Aiken. I truly am." He kissed her again. "I'll be back as soon as I can."

"Corbin, be careful!" There were tears in her eyes.

He leaped over the guardrail and jogged along the

dock for the *Columbia's* berth. "I'll be all right!" he called. "We'll talk later."

He slowed as he neared the boat. Corbin hopped up on its port deck and straddled the lifeline. He stepped down into the cockpit, leaned over toward the sail locker and raised it.

The jib's storage bag lay where he had stowed it earlier; but as he peered around the locker, he could not locate the dinghy.

"Every second counts," he mumbled. "Where is it?"

"Calm down! 'Some things are in our power and some things are not!' " he quoted the old Stoic adage to himself.

But is this in my power? he wondered.

"Yes!" he assured himself.

Corbin once again surveyed the compartment's contents. Suddenly, he saw it. The dinghy lay beneath the storage bag. It was folded neatly where Aiken had stowed it in a large green canvas sack. The raft's plywood accordion floor and a foot pump lay tucked beside the big bag, and beneath the floor lay the oars.

Corbin had to lie on his stomach to reach the bag. Its reinforced cord handles were difficult to clasp, but he managed to haul it up, along with its accordion floor and foot pump. He laid the pump and floor on the bench behind him and dragged the bag toward the galley. He pulled out the inflatable dinghy and wrestled it up on the hatch. Corbin unfolded it and began to screw in its air valves. Then he placed the floorboard in it, unfolded the board's three sections, and tucked each corner in its proper fold.

Now to inflate it! he thought.

He returned to the bench for the pump, climbed up on the hatch, and fastened the pump's hose to the right intake valve. He screwed it on tightly and began working the billows with his right foot.

As soon as he had inflated the right hemisphere, he secured its valve; he unscrewed the hose and threaded it on to the second valve. This time he pumped with his left foot and soon had it filled. He was now ready to launch it.

Corbin dragged the big raft off the hatch and down into the cockpit. He wedged it momentarily between the two seats; he turned about, bent down over the locker, and drew the oars up through the opening. Corbin slid the dinghy carefully off the back of the transom into the water. He laid the oars in it and inched down the ladder slowly. In his hand he clutched a red cord that was affixed to a patch on the dinghy.

Corbin lowered himself gingerly into the raft and squatted comfortably enough on the bottom. He fitted each oar into its lock and pushed cleanly but cautiously away from the *Columbia*.

All this had required time. "Valuable time!" he acknowledge to himself.

He glanced over his left shoulder to square off his course, then applied his back and arms to his task, and began rowing toward the entrance into the channel.

"You can still make it!" he told himself. "Just pull! Pull! Pull!"

chapter **twenty**

Rowing out into the channel went more quickly than Corbin thought it would.

"Perhaps that is a good omen!" he told himself. "Please, be there!" he whispered aloud, hoping that the *Rubi-Yacht* was still afloat.

He rowed steadily, hard, and rhythmically, first past the lily pads and then past each channel marker. From time to time he glanced over his shoulder, but he could not see the *Rubi-Yacht*.

"It has to be there!" he said. "It can't have gone down that quickly."

"Please! Where are you?" he whispered.

The rain had lifted now and much of the darker cloud cover had dissipated with it. A steamy mist had settled upon the cove. Far across the lake, a stream of pale sunlight struggled to beam its way through the tattered remnants of the storm.

A brisk breeze moved upon the water and stirred the warm mist. But the breeze felt cold to Corbin.

He was clad only in his knit shirt and tan shorts and was still barefoot and wet. Goose bumps quivered on his arms and on the upper portion of his thighs.

All across the cove, water undulated in choppy waves. It splashed against the dinghy and up onto Corbin's clothes. Corbin could hear it lapping against the shore, beyond the lily pads.

Then he saw the *Rubi-Yacht!* It had drifted eastward across the cove. Its hull lay lodged against the rocks along the causeway; its mast and rigging were tossing to and fro, as the boat jostled back and forth, rocked by the motion of the incoming wakes. The cockpit wallowed from side to side, almost submerged; the galley appeared flooded. Only the hatch, foredeck, and mast poked out of the water.

More than ever now, Corbin strained against the oars.

More than ever now, Corbin wanted to reach his boat.

More than ever now, Corbin wanted to hold that picture. To put his hands up to that photograph one last time. To save it, if possible!

He rowed until his hands began to bleed.

Until the blood stuck to the oars.

Until his back ached, and his side began to hurt again, where he had struck it earlier while launching the *Rubi-Yacht.*

"Please! Please!" he whispered.

"Please!" he pulled.

"Please!" he repeated.

He looked about. There it lay.

He could hear its hull grinding against the rocks.

And the waves splashing upon the foredeck.

There was a loud groaning sound, and the boat slipped beneath the water; it came to rest with only the tip of its pulpit protruding above the swells.

He knew it would not remain there long.

What thou must do, do quickly! he thought.

He laid the oars along the lip of the dinghy and rolled sideways, into the water. Everything rose upside-down, as he did. He came up to the surface and inhaled a huge gulp of air, then dove under, and began groping his way toward the hull.

It was dark in the water and cold. Only the thinnest rays of light illumined his craft. He swam past the dark rocks and glided closer to the galley. He pulled himself deeper toward its entrance and peered inside the cabin. An air bubble loomed trapped along the starboard wall, near the forward bulkhead. He squirmed his way into the cabin, swam up toward the air bubble, and inhaled a deep breath. Its mildewed taste stung his lungs, but he scarcely cared.

Corbin resubmerged and groped his way to the photograph. He ran his fingers across the glass and about the frame. If only he had not secured it so well!

He glanced quickly about, for any instrument he might use to break the glass. But none seemed available. He pulled his way over to the cabinet and searched for a knife. He found one and felt his way back to the photograph.

His lungs burned. His nostrils began trailing tiny bubbles of rapidly escaping air.

I can still do it, he thought, as he rose up to the trapped bubble for a second inhalation.

Once more he returned to the picture; he wedged the knife blade between the frame and the wall and pried gently against the picture. But nothing budged. He applied pressure again and snapped the blade. He beat on the glass with the handle, cracked it, but could not slide the broken pieces out.

Suddenly, the vessel shifted and rolled starboard slightly, taking Corbin with it. The bubble of trapped air gurgled and disappeared out the cabin and into the water.

Corbin swam back to the photograph and ran his fingers affectionately across the two faces.

"I must go now," he whispered to them, "though I shall hate it all the days of my life."

He leaned toward Janet's image and kissed her lips.

"You must go!" she suddenly whispered.

"I know," he answered, as he ran his hands across

the photo, taking in its blurred images for the last time.

"Craig will always be with you. And I too, in your heart."

"Yes, darling, I know."

"Go, now!" she urged him. "Before it is too late. Wherever you are, I will be with you. Whenever you remember me, I will be there. Let me kiss you one more time. And go. Please, Corbin! Go!"

"Yes," he repeated.

"I love you, Corbin. Oh, darling, how I loved you!"

"Yes, I loved you too. I loved you with all my soul."

"O darling! Good bye!"

"Good-bye!" he kissed her, trailing his fingertips across the photograph for the last time.

He turned and cast the knife's handle aside. He watched it somersault dreamlike in the darkness of the cabin. Then he kicked off. Just as he did, his right foot struck the table's leg, causing it to fold in, and the table top to sway up and collapse tightly against his foot.

He tugged at his ankle, but his foot was caught. It was wedged, trapped. Large bubbles of air escaped from his lips in a steady stream. His nose burned; his lungs felt on the verge of explosion.

Suddenly, the boat groaned and began settling again.

"Thou art not going to make it."

"Yes, I am!" Corbin retorted. "I must, for Janet's sake. For Craig's."

"No thou aren't! Thou art not in command here."

Just then a shadow appeared outside the hull. A movement, swimming alongside and toward the cabin.

Corbin pulled again on his foot, but to no avail.

The shadow drew closer. Suddenly, an arm protruded into the galley and a dark face behind it.

It was God Boy!

So Death had sent God Boy. How clever of Death, thought Corbin.

"O God Boy! Can we not wait a while!" he whispered. "Please! Just one more chance," he said, as he tugged at his foot.

But God Boy pulled past the entrance and groped for him with his hands. He seized him by the shoulders and pulled himself inside.

"God Boy! Please! I am losing consciousness! Not now. Please, not now! Can't you see you are only playing into Death's hands? Please, God Boy! Don't end it all now!"

But God Boy wrestled past Corbin's struggling arms, swam to the collapsed table, and raised it off his leg. Slowly, he turned, gathered Corbin under his right arm, and began forcing him through the entrance and out of the galley.

Corbin tried to block God Boy's passage. "No! Thou shalt not take me!" his words bubbled in the water. "Not now! No!"

A paroxysm of pain exploded in Corbin's lungs. His head and chest began jerking with convulsions. His eyes burned; his strength failed, and the light in his mind became as dark. Corbin bowed his head, and his spirit floated free of his body.

It was like a dream. His mind was still conscious, yet he knew he was dead. He could see his body limp in the water and God Boy ferrying him along, as if the old Captain were dragging a submerged cargo through the water.

A thin stream of iridescence illumined a murky path toward which God Boy now turned.

Corbin's spirit waned. Darkness came down upon his soul.

It is finished! he thought, as the image of Janet and Craig flickered across his heart and the voice of Jil called to him in the dark.

chapter **twenty-one**

And when the deed was done and back swam he,
We fetched him leeward from the reeling sea,
And rolled him in a canvas, for quite dead was
  he,
And we hove him in the Lowland, Lowland,
  low,
And hove him in the Lowland Sea.

Somewhere a gull cried in the darkness, its high cluck lingering in the silent wake of its flight. Waves sloshed against a rocking hull, and the faint sound of a tocsin rattled in the night.

A fire burned with wavering coals and trickles of pain flickered at the center of the burning. The smell of bile and vomit hovered in the air. Hushed voices whispered in the darkness.

Why dost thou rouse me from this slumber? And from the numbing coils of death's night?

"Harmond, his lips are moving! I think he's breathing again!"

There was the sound of coughing, mingled with the sweet odor of vomit and the taste of bile.

"O Corbin! He's going to make it! Harmond, he's going to make it!"

"Thank God," wafted a coarse whisper on the air. "He fought me long enough. Ah, I am tired!"

The softness of arms and the smell of hair encompassed the fading dark. The warmth of the sun had rubbed the night away.

"Jil! Jil!" Corbin coughed. He opened his eyes and stared at the dark images around him and tried to clear the burning from his throat. "It was so dark! So cold!"

He was trembling and quivering. He groped for Jil's hands, searching for her fingers with his own, with the softened raw edges of his oar-blistered water-withered palms.

"Corbin!" she bent down to kiss him and pressed her bosom against his cold wet chest.

"Do you see the light?" he coughed, spitting up and swallowing back trickles of hot bile.

"Yes! Yes, darling!"

"It was so dark. So dark!"

"Yes, darling. Yes!" she whispered, kissing her hot tears off his clammy watery cheeks.

He clasped her hand and placed it to his lips, then put his arm about her waist. "I'm sorry about Aiken.

God, darling, but I am."

"Yes," she murmured, cradling him in her arms, as Harmond pulled on the sputtering outboard and motored the *Columbia* toward the harbor, thumping the boat softly and rhythmically through the cold stinging spray.

"I thought you were dead."

"I thought I was too," he said as he struggled to raise his head. He held her face against his neck, so that she could not see his eyes. And he remembered the stars. Janet. God Boy. Aiken. And the *Rubi-Yacht.*

Glossary of Sailing Terms

Binnacle: A nonmagnetic stand on which a boat's compass is displayed.

Boom: A long pole-like member hinged to a fixture low on the aft side of the mast. The hinge (called a "gooseneck") permits lateral movement of the boom.

Cleat: A metal fitting with two projecting horns around which a line (rope) may be made fast.

Close hauled: A course of sail with respect to wind direction. In a close haul heading, a sailboat is said to be sailing as nearly as practicable toward the point from which the wind is blowing.

Foredeck: The forward part of a boat's main deck, usually the deck area forward of the mast.

Forecastle: The section of bunk space below the foredeck, frequently called the "vee bunk."

Genoa: An oversized jib that overlaps the mainsail.

Halyard: A line (rope) for raising a sail.

Jib: A triangular sail set forward of the mast with its leading edge (the luff) clipped or hanked on the forestay.

Mainsail: A triangular sail mounted on the aft side of the mast with the foot (the part of a sail closest to the deck) of the sail stretched along the boom.

Port: The left side of a boat when one faces forward.

Sheet: A line (rope) attached to the lower and aftermost corner of a sail. Sheets are employed by the sailor to achieve optimum sail shape for given wind and sea conditions.

Shroud lines: Wire cables (usually stainless steel) rigged across the boat under tension, from one side of the boat to the masthead and back down to the other side. At each end cables are securely held fast with fixtures known as chain plates.

Sliding hatch: A hatch to cover or uncover an opening in a sailboat's cabin roof. The sliding hatch together with the boat's hatchboards protect the companionway when such hatches are employed.

Sloop: A sailboat rigged fore and aft with one mast well forward.

Spreaders: Spars or struts positioned high on a boat's mast, one to starboard and one to port. Spreaders are rigged to hold apart two or more shroud lines.

Starboard: The right side of the boat when one faces forward.

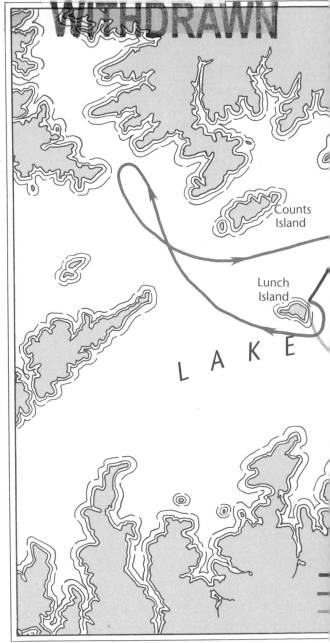

Counts
Island

Lunch
Island

L A K E